Triplecross Trail

The Lost Treasure Ship of the Mojave, said to be loaded with a cargo of black pearls from the Sea of Cortez, was probably the oldest, most persistent tale of lost treasure in the West.

Ned Gamble, a down-at-heel drifter, is hired to guide a high-class Mexican woman into the Yuha Badlands in search of the ancient vessel and finds instead that he's stumbled into a game of treachery and triple-cross.

Still, unravelling the legend of the ancient ship would make a man rich as a king . . . if it doesn't kill him first.

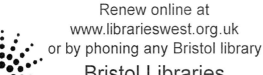

Triplecross Trail

Josh Lockwood

A Black Horse Western

ROBERT HALE · LONDON

ISBN 978-0-7198-0976-7

Robert Hale Limited
Clerkenwell House
Clerkenwell Green
London EC1R 0HT

www.halebooks.com

Typeset by
Derek Doyle & Associates, Shaw Heath
Printed and bound in Great Britain by
CPI Antony Rowe, Chippenham and Eastbourne

CHAPTER ONE

Of course he'd heard the story.

Anyone who'd sat around as many campfires as he had was bound to sooner or later. It was probably the oldest, most persistent tale of lost treasure in the West, except maybe for that whopper about the Lost Dutchman mine up there in the Superstitions.

Still, it surprised the hell out of him when that hidalgo-looking woman started talking about it.

He'd just trailed into Yuma with six of the finest Morgan horses he'd ever seen and had an idea that maybe he could start a horse ranch over on the coast. There was some likely-looking land north of Los Angeles and the Morgans would be a damned good start.

It was a shot, anyway.

He was sitting quietly in the shadowed dining room of the old Frontier Hotel, the sun just going down, and all of a sudden the well-dressed Mexican woman at the corner table stood up, sauntered across the room, and asked if she could join him.

Her long, raven hair swayed slightly as she walked: a man could have drowned in her eyes and there he sat, all dusty and worn out, hungry, and tired from the ride. The air of the dining room was heavy with the aroma of fresh-baked bread and searing steaks and, even with that, he could smell the faint aroma of soap when she approached.

'You're Ned Gamble?' she asked softly.

He glanced up at the voice and knew right off he'd made his first mistake.

A soft smile quirked her lips and she seemed to be a little embarrassed at her own boldness.

Still, there was something in the way she carried herself that spoke of elegance, of upbringing, and that was a rare thing in a ramshackle town like Yuma.

'Was when I shaved this morning.'

'Would you mind if I join you?' she asked. 'I understand you know your way around the desert.'

'I've been out there a time or two.'

Tired as he was, he rose to his full height, pulled out a chair, and nodded for her to sit down.

'What can I do for you?'

She lowered herself into the rickety cane chair, glanced cautiously around the room, and took her own sweet time about answering. She ordered a cup of tea for herself and a refill on his coffee, then just sat there sizing him up with those big, flashing black eyes of hers.

And he didn't know if he'd passed muster or not.

After a long moment of studying him with those disturbing eyes, she spoke. 'I'm looking for someone to lead me into the desert.'

'And you are?'

'The name is Dolores Torreón, Mr Gamble. I was told you were on your way here and I've been waiting for you for some time.'

'Who gave you that information?'

'A Mr Frank Dougherty at the livery stable.'

Well, that was the first time any woman who didn't have a crib on the second floor of a saloon somewhere had spoken to him in a couple of months, and he just wasn't sure what the occasion was. Beat up as he was right then, he felt pretty sure he wasn't anything special to look at.

'Any particular place you want to go out there?'

'Yes,' she said evenly. 'As a matter of fact, I'm looking for a treasure ship.'

And that was just about all he could handle for one day.

He'd been in the desert too long, hadn't had a decent meal or heard a human voice for three weeks, and that hidalgo-looking woman was going to sit there and throw legends in his face?

'Let me guess,' he rumbled over the rim of his cup. 'You've got a map that you bought from a gentleman in Santa Fe, and he guaranteed it would lead you to the Lost Treasure Ship of the Mojave.

'He would have gone himself but he has tuberculosis, needs money for his medicine, and that's the only reason he's selling the map.'

He took another swig of his coffee, wishing to hell it was something stronger, and raked her with his eyes.

'My best guess would be that there are about ten thousand of those things floating around the West by now,' he said in a coarse whisper. 'Seems like every confidence man from Saint Louis to San Francisco has one to sell.'

She wagged her head in despair at the bitterness in his voice but didn't look away.

'You must think me an absolute fool,' she said across the table. 'No, I don't have a treasure map, sir. I have something better. Much better.'

And, with that, she reached inside a heavy handbag she was carrying and pulled out a small, leather-bound book.

'I have the original of Father Venegas's manuscript, giving very detailed information as to the ship's location.'

He stared at her for a long minute then, on edge and not quite sure what was coming next. Her face was in shadow and he could read nothing at all in her expression.

'What do you mean, "the original"?'

She kept her voice low, glancing warily around the room as if she were afraid of being overheard. 'The work was modified some time after it was written by a Father Andrés Burriel, supposedly taking out all the dubious material and restricting the account only to well-documented voyages.

'The simple truth of the matter is, however, the Franciscan order they belonged to didn't want the information it contained falling into hands outside the church. It took me three years of digging through the musty vaults of Mexico City to find it.'

'All right if I look at it?' he asked tilting his head toward the book.

'Of course it is,' she said softly, 'but only you.' And, with a flick of her wrist, she slid the book toward him.

It was an old damned thing – really, really old – and he half expected the calfskin binding to fall apart in his hands when he picked it up. He squinted at the title that had been stamped across the cover in flaky gold leaf lettering.

Noticia de la California y de su conquista temporal y espiritual hasta el tiempo presente. Sacada de la historia manuscrita, formada en Mexico año de 1739 por el Padre Miguel Venegas de la Compania de Jesus.

'I speak a little Spanish,' he said, narrowing his eyes at her, 'but I'll need some help with this.'

'Certainly,' she replied with the hint of a smile quaking her lips. 'It says: News of California and its temporal and spiritual conquest to the present time. Taken from the history manuscript, formed in Mexico in 1739 by Father Miguel Venegas of the Society of Jesus.'

He thumbed it open and glanced at a couple of pages. All in Spanish, of course, looking as if it had been written with one of those old quill pens. Big fancy penmanship, flourishes all over the place and very heavy letters.

He set it back down within her reach, took

another sip of coffee, and studied her.

He'd seen women like her before, daughters and mistresses of those big plantation owners back in the Carolinas during the war, and knew exactly what she represented.

She was wealth, extravagance, leisure; she was never having to get her hands dirty, never doing an honest day's work in her life, and, strangely enough, he had no liking for her.

'And this is supposed to be genuine?'

'Oh, believe me,' she purred, 'it's genuine.'

'Well, I'll be damned.'

'I take it you've heard the story, then?'

'All three versions of it, miss,' he answered. 'Over lonely campfires at night. The first version has it that it was a fifty-ton Spanish caravel, loaded with black pearls from the Sea of Cortez, which sailed up into Lake Cahuilla and couldn't get back out.'

'Captain Juan de Iturbe's ship,' she chimed in.

He shrugged at her words and went on. 'The second version is that of a Viking ship, a serpent-necked canoe anyway, with shields fastened to the gunwales, and the third is that it was nothing more than a Colorado River ferryboat that had been abandoned out there.'

She met his gaze evenly across the table then, apparently satisfied she'd found someone who really did know his way around the desert.

'And which version of the story do you favor?' she asked with a tilt of her head.

He huffed quietly at her question. It was like

asking a man whether he believed in Santa Claus or the Tooth Fairy.

'I'm not so sure I favor any of them,' he said, 'but I would tend to think the Juan de Iturbe story makes the most sense, considering the time.'

'There's also the story of Tiburcio Manquerna, Mr Gamble,' she ventured. 'Have you heard that one?'

'Not that I recall,' he said tiredly, 'but I have the strangest feeling you're going to tell it to me.'

'I will if you're interested.'

'Sure, why not? I don't have anything better to do this evening.'

She took a small sip of tea, cleared her throat, and tented her fingers above the table.

'Tiburcio Manquerna was a mule driver with Juan Bautista de Anza on his search to find a land route from Sonora to Alta California, Mr Gamble, and he claimed he'd been sent to the right of de Anza's course, seeking the road to the ocean.

'He said he was traveling by night because of the heat when he stumbled upon an ancient ship, and in its hold were so many pearls as were beyond imagination.

'Fevered by the wealth, he said he took what he could carry, abandoned his comrades, and rode toward the ocean as far as his mule could carry him. He claimed that he climbed the western mountains on foot, fed by the local Indians, and at last reached the mission of San Luis and from there returned to Mexico. They say he spent the rest of his life trying to find the ship again and never did.'

11

Ned just gave her a big, stupid grin.

'That'd be a great story to tell over a campfire, lady,' he muttered. 'Nobody'd believe it for a minute, but it would be a great one to tell.'

The look that spread across her face then said she was not happy with his response.

'What would it take to convince you it was true?'

'Well, I don't know,' he said, 'but I'm thinking it would have to be something a little more substantial than a free cup of coffee in a dusty dining room.'

Without another word she reached into a pocket of her grey traveling dress and laid her fist in the center of the table; he started hearing tiny clicking sounds, as if she were tapping the table with her fingernails.

When she pulled her hand back there were six lustrous black pearls sitting on the marred tabletop, glowing seductively in the dim lanternlight of the room.

'Is that substantial enough?'

He sat up straight in his chair then, completely mesmerized by the display of pearls; he opened his mouth to speak, but no words came out.

'Tiburcio Manquerna was my great-great-grandfather, Mr Gamble,' she said, nodding toward the pearls. 'He brought home a great many of those when he came back from Alta California. My family sold them off a few at a time to finance their ranch in Jalisco.

'The land was confiscated a few years ago by the Porfirio Díaz government and we've been getting by, living on the proceeds of selling the pearls, ever since. These six are all that are left.'

It dawned on him then – like a revelation from God – that the woman was dead serious about all this.

'And you think there are more of them out there?'

'I *know* there are more of them out there, *señor*,' she said. 'A great many more. Enough to make the both of us very, very wealthy. All we have to do is find them.'

Yeah, just that easy.

All we have to do is find them.

'Are you kidding me, lady?' he blurted. 'Have you got any idea in the world how big the Mojave Desert is? How little water is out there? How deep the sand?'

Of course, she didn't respond.

It didn't surprise him. Anyone could tell, just by looking at her, that she had no idea what she was talking about. She just wasn't a desert type of woman.

No, sir.

She'd have been a great one to have on your arm strolling around the town plaza on a quiet Sunday afternoon, but not the kind a man would want with him in the desert.

He'd have bet money on the barrelhead she couldn't cook or even carry water. Just someone really pretty to look at.

But she had that damned book!

That damned little book written by a Franciscan padre a century and a half before, with very detailed information as to the ship's location in it.

And she wasn't about to give up.

She was used to having things her own way, accustomed to being waited on hand and foot, accustomed to giving orders, and Ned had the feeling deep down inside himself that men couldn't say 'no' to her.

She would just bat her eyes or give them that soft smile of hers, and they'd melt like cow's butter on an August day.

Anything she wanted. Carry my trunk, a cup of tea, anything at all. If she asked, it was done, and the man walked away feeling like he'd died and gone to heaven.

'I'll pay you two hundred dollars and give you half the pearls we recover if you guide me out there,' she said quietly.

Now that was a sight of money she was offering. Way more than he'd ever make selling horses in California.

Definitely an offer worth considering.

'I'd be getting the better end of the deal,' he mumbled.

She shrugged her softly rounded shoulders then and cocked her head. 'I know your reputation, *señor*. Without you guiding me, there may be no pearls at all.'

'Things have a way of changing in the desert, miss,' he offered. 'Earthquakes, windstorms, flash

14

floods. There's every chance in the world that what we'd find out there won't match the description you have in that book.'

'But it's worth the risk if we do find it.'

He couldn't argue with that. He knew full well there were men in Yuma – right there in the hotel dining room, for that matter – who would kill for nothing more than the pearls sitting on the table, and others who would kill for nothing more than the information she claimed to have in that little book.

'When would you want to leave?'

She grimaced at his question. 'The sooner the better.'

'First light?' he asked.

'Yes, I can be ready by then.'

He nodded, threw down the rest of his coffee and pushed himself up. 'Good enough. I'll meet you at the ferry landing first thing in the morning. Be ready for a long day's ride.'

He ambled away from the table, into the hotel's barroom, and found an empty spot at the counter.

The bartender, a scarecrow of a man with a protruding Adam's apple, stopped in front of him, wiped the bar with a damp rag, and flapped the rag over his shoulder. 'What can I get for you?'

'Rye whiskey if you've got any.' Ned slid a dollar coin on to the bar and continued. 'You can just leave the bottle.'

'Good-lookin' female you was talkin' to in there.'

'Yeah,' Ned replied, 'but I don't think she's my type.'

'Any woman's my type.' The barkeep grinned. 'The worst I ever had was wonderful.'

CHAPTER TWO

Ned had some serious pondering to do.

He'd never had much in the way of worldly possessions: a good horse, a fairly new rifle, and a big Colt Peacemaker. Things he knew he could rely on. Still he had that fragment of thought in his mind about raising horses in California, figuring it might build into some kind of a future for him.

And this little venture with the Torreón woman meant putting that dream on hold for God knew how long and scrabbling around in the desert with a female who very likely didn't know horse apples from Gila monsters.

First of all, he doubted she'd be able to handle the heat out there. Maybe on a shaded veranda somewhere with a cool drink in her hand, but not in the Yuha badlands.

She just wasn't the type.

He walked the horses down to the livery stable, paid old Frank to feed and grain them, bought a big

sorrel mare and a used saddle for the Mex woman –
wasn't about to risk his Morgans out there – bought
grub for the trail at the general store, and got
himself a room for the night at the Frontier.

But, tired as he was, sleep wouldn't come.

He lay there half the night staring at the water
stained ceiling and considering the whole deal.

He knew a little more of the story than the
Torreón woman did in spite of all her research and
digging through the musty vaults of Mexico City,
only he'd kept it to himself.

He never had been much on trusting folks.

A couple of winters ago he'd met an old Cahuilla
warrior from the Agua Caliente band over there in
California. He called himself Huarache – Spanish
for sandal – and he'd told Ned a story handed down
from his grandfather's grandfather, the way he put
it, that kind of fitted in with all this talk of inland
seas and sailing ships.

The story was that the first time the Cahuilla
people had seen a white man they'd come on a great
white bird, floating in from down Mexico way.

In Ned's mind that great white bird of theirs could
just as easily have been a ship under sail.

Hell, the Indians had never seen a ship and he
thought it likely that the first time they did they
might equate it to something they were familiar with
. . . like some big, ungainly bird.

It made sense to him, anyway.

Huarache had told him the great white bird had
come to a hill and stopped, the water went away, and

the bird was in the sand. He said the white bird stayed down there for a long, long time, then its wings fell off and sand covered it up.

The way Ned had it figured, if he could locate old Huarache again and have him point out the hill he'd told him about – plus all the information that hidalgo-looking woman had in that book of hers – they might actually pull this thing off.

She was offering a sight of money for him to take her out there.

It would be hard to pass on a deal like that.

He rolled out at first light, groggy from lack of sleep, wandered down to the livery stable and caught old Frank just as he was pouring his first cup of coffee.

'I'm guessing that Torreón woman talked you into taking her out there,' the old man mumbled.

'Yeah,' Ned said, rinsing out one of Frank's dented cups. 'She's got a way with words.'

Frank chuckled, half under his breath. 'And that ain't all she's got, *hombre*. I want you to watch your topknot while you're out there, you hear?'

'Why's that?'

The ageing hostler cocked his head and glanced up from the corners of his eyes. The suspicion in them was plain to see.

'There were six *vaqueros* followed her into town when she first showed up, Ned. Evil-looking characters. And they've been watching every move she makes since she got here. Their horses are stabled in back but I don't recognize any of the brands, you

19

know? Not from around here, that's for damned sure.'

Ned splashed the steaming hot coffee into his cup, the aroma teasing his nostrils, and glanced back up.

'And what does all that mean to me?'

'That I'm not sure of, my friend, but seems to me it's more than a passing interest. I just thought you should know.'

'Any names?' he asked.

'Just one . . . Manny Barajas . . . but that don't ring any bells, either.'

Ned nodded his understanding. 'Appreciate the information, Frank,' he told him. 'I'll keep my eyes open.'

'You do that,' Dougherty mumbled. 'I'd hate to lose one of my regular customers.'

Frank was one of the old time mountain men who'd tamed the West – fought Indians, blizzards, and droughts all the way from Montana to the Sierra Madres with not much more than a gun and a whole lot of courage – and he had a sort of sixth sense about people.

You couldn't call it first impressions, really, although he did form his opinions pretty quick. It was more of an ingrained thing with him.

He'd look a man over, listen to his manner of speaking, watch the way he carried himself – a puma on the prowl or a tabby cat looking for a bowl of milk – and could pretty much tell where his stick floated.

He was seldom wrong and, if you knew old Frank

at all, you knew enough to listen when he spoke.

And Ned? He knew Frank pretty damned well.

The old liveryman excused himself and got on with his daily routine of tending the horses under his care. Ned stared after him, considering what he'd just been told.

None of it made much sense. Brands from out of the area, a name neither one of them knew. There had to be a reason these *vaqueros* were watching the woman, and not knowing that reason gave him pause.

He shrugged off his unease. There wasn't much he could do about it either way. He set the cup on Frank's cluttered desk, eased on back to the stables, and saddled the grulla mare he ride.

It took only a few more minutes to load the supplies on to the dapple-grey packhorse, and he shoved one of Frank's scoop shovels in under the pack straps, just in case.

Ned swung up into the saddle, tossed an offhand two-fingered salute to the old guy, and trailed out toward the ferry landing.

A wave of surprise washed over him that the Torreón woman was even down there that early in the morning, but she was.

She stood quietly by one of the tall masts jutting up beside the landing into the dry desert air.' She was all decked out in a maroon skirt, a spotless white blouse, and looking as if she was ready for a carriage ride from her family's ranch in Jalisco to the big city.

She handed him a big leather *aparejo* with God

21

knew what all in it to load on the packhorse, then he had to help her up on to the sorrel. And, when she swung up, she hooked one knee around the pommel as if she were riding a sidesaddle.

It was then that the reality of the whole shebang hit him.

He was in for a seriously hard time for the next week or so and he knew it.

He was going to be doing it all out there – tending the horses, gathering wood, building the fire, cooking the food – while she sat around looking pretty and reading that damned little book of hers.

He was walking into it with his eyes wide open.

Dumber'n a sack full of rocks.

'You don't have a sombrero?' he asked. 'Some kind of wide-brimmed hat?'

'I have a parasol,' she said, smiling down at him. 'That should be sufficient.'

He wagged his head at her words. 'You haven't spent much time in the desert, have you, miss?'

'That was always the men's work. Rounding up cattle and the like.'

Ned lifted his hands in resignation, led the horses aboard the ferry, and watched as the crewmen started heaving on the long rope that had been strung across the muddy Colorado River.

'You got our horses ready, old man?'

Frank Dougherty lifted his gaze from the sack of oats he was opening, not accustomed to being spoken to with such open contempt and not liking it for a Mexican minute. He turned his head slightly and spat tobacco juice into the straw that covered the stable floor in front of the *vaquero*.

'Nobody said a word about having your horses ready, mister, and I'll thank you to keep a civil damned tongue in your head.'

'A civil tongue?' the *vaquero* scoffed loudly. 'You make me laugh. We are men of action. We have no need of civil tongues.'

'And I have two-bit toughs like you for breakfast. Saddle your own goddamned horses.'

The heavyset *vaquero* grinned wryly at Frank's words. He jammed his heavy Colt Army into the old hostler's midsection and coughed laughter in his face.

'Here, old man,' he rumbled as he pulled the trigger, 'you can have this for breakfast, too.'

The gunshot was muffled slightly by Frank's girth and he stumbled back against the stable's rough-sawn wall, clutching at his stomach, his face twisted by the searing pain of the shot.

'You sonofabitch,' he croaked. 'You didn't have to do that.'

The *vaquero* squeezed the trigger a second time, a little higher, and Frank went down for good, a bloody heap in the straw.

'Just as well,' Manny Barajas said from the door. '*Pendejos* like that wear on me.'

He turned slightly, wiping a blunt thumb across his neatly trimmed mustache, and bobbed his head at his men. 'Paco, round up the horses that gringo brought with him. They'll bring a good price in Los Angeles.'

'Los Angeles?'

'*Sí*. That's where we're going. We'll take a ship back to Acapulco.'

Almost as one his men nodded their agreement with his plan and he continued, handing a fistful of coins to the man standing next to him.

'Miguelito, swing by the general store and get us some food for the trail. Tortillas and beans, chorizos and rice. Get a few bottles of mezcal, too. Whatever you think we need. Then meet us at the landing.'

'Get me a sack of tobacco while you're there,' Paco added.

'Indio,' Barajas continued, 'I want you to go across now. Keep Dolores and the gringo in sight, but raise no dust. I don't want them to know they're being followed. It will be our ace in the hole. You can report back to me at sunset.'

He stood silent for a moment then, eyeing his small band. '*Vamonos, muchachos*! We're wasting time.'

The new man in his group, a slender half-breed known only as Indio, ducked his head at their leader and broke his silence. 'You think this gringo can really find the pearls, Manny?'

Barajas made a dubious face at his question. 'He has the reputation of knowing the desert. If anyone can find them, it will be him.'

'We'll be rich,' the 'breed muttered.

24

'Just don't get careless out there, Indio. The man also has the reputation of being a fierce fighter.'

The dark water hissed and boiled against the ferry's bluff side, slopping up on to the deck in places, making the horses chuff and stamp their hoofs in nervousness. The groan of the cables straining through the huge wooden blocks on the landing came to them all the way across the river.

The relentless current pushed the barge downstream until the heavy hawser anchored in the landings would give no more; it then tipped awkwardly, the crewmen still heaving on the line, and they inched their way very slowly through the torrent to the other side.

Dolores Torreón reined in the moment they rode off the craft, sat her horse at the side of the rutted wagon road, and took a long, critical look at the countryside around them.

'So this is California.'

'The bitter end of it,' Ned told her, glancing around at the mesquite beside the road. 'It improves over toward the coast.'

'Amazing.' She sighed. 'So this is where my great-great-grandfather crossed into Alta California all those years ago.'

'It is if he was with de Anza.'

'Oh, he was with de Anza, all right. There is absolutely no doubt about that. I just find it strange to be in the exact same spot after all this time.'

'All right if I call you Dolores?' he asked.

Her eyes went wide, as if she couldn't quite believe her ears. 'Well, of course it is. That is my name, after all. And I shall call you Ned.'

He nodded and studied her for a brief moment. 'That sounds better than being called Mr Gamble every time you speak. Makes it sound like I'm some kind of big businessman from back East somewhere, and I'm not. I'm just an ordinary guy getting by the best I know how.'

'And how do you get by?' she asked quietly.

He snorted at her question. 'I've been banging around the West for a long time, miss. I've done everything from pick-and-shovel mining to driving for Wells Fargo, and damn me if I still ain't living on bacon and beans.'

'Then this could be your big chance.'

'Could be,' he said. 'If we find anything.'

He swung up into the saddle, nodded toward the west, and nudged the mare into a ground-eating canter.

Following the rutted wagon road in silence, they worked their way through the wide mesquite thicket just south of the Quartermaster Depot on the hill above the river, crossed the tail end of the bleak Algodones Dunes, and skirted Pilot Knob before the heat of the day really set in.

The sky was cloudless, as it normally was at that time of year, and the air was heavy with the cloying tar-and-orange-blossom fragrance of the creosote bushes.

'This whole area was under water at one time,' he

26

said, sweeping his hand at the mud hills and sage-covered flats to the north and west.

'Really?' she asked, arching her eyebrows.

'Oh, yeah,' he answered easily. 'To the north there, you can find whole beds of oyster shells and, on over toward the mountains, there are even some ancient coral reefs.'

'Amazing,' she murmured. 'You'd never know it by looking.'

'Not unless you look at it close. If all this stuff about Juan de Iturbe is true, this would be just about where he sailed in.'

She tilted her head, squinting at him in the gathering heat of the flats. 'Now that really *is* amazing. I had no idea.'

They rode on then, walking the horses to spare them, paying little attention to the shimmering heat waves around them or the black curves of turkey vultures wheeling in great, lazy circles high above their heads.

He felt the perspiration trickling down his back beneath the shirt and had to wipe the sweatband of his hat over and over again.

There was no shelter from the relentless low desert sun when Ned finally reined in beside the trail for a nooning. He gave each horse a scant hatful of water from the canteens, put together a small fire of mesquite branches, and set his smoke-blackened coffee pot down on a chunk of rock to heat up.

He handed Dolores a few pieces of venison jerky and one of his dented tin cups. 'Coffee will be ready in a few minutes,' he told her, 'or there's water in the canteen if you prefer that.'

'I'll wait for the coffee. We drink a lot of that at home.'

'Your choice,' he replied, 'but don't start considering this place your home. You don't belong out here.'

'I'm not so sure about that. People say I fit in anywhere.'

'That's not what I meant and you know it.'

He lowered himself to the speckled gravel, wiped the sweatband of his hat with his ragged blue bandanna yet again, and studied a dust plume lifting into the air several miles back along the trail.

'There are people behind us,' he murmured. 'I've been seeing their dust for a couple of hours now and they don't seem to be in any hurry.'

'People?'

'Yeah. That's way too much dust for a single rider. My guess would be half a dozen or so.'

She frowned. 'Do you think they're following us?'

'I doubt it,' he said. 'This is a pretty well-traveled trail. I imagine we'll find out at the well tonight. Yuha Well is the first reliable water hole this side of the river. Sixty, sixty-five miles west of Yuma.'

'Is that where we're going?'

'We don't have much choice, miss. And whoever's behind us doesn't have much choice, either. Only an absolute fool would pass up a chance for water out here.'

'Or someone who doesn't want to be seen?' she ventured.

He narrowed his eyes and peered at the dust plume again.

He hadn't even considered that.

CHAPTER THREE

The mesquite-covered hummock that marked Yuha Well was visible from several miles out on the creosote-covered flats.

Aside from the thicket itself there was no shelter to be had from either the elements or attack and he had never felt comfortable camping there.

They rode in slowly, Ned eyeing the site for a decent spot to pitch camp and reading the ground for sign of any recent activity.

He ducked his head toward a fairly flat shelf of gravel a little away from the water, tugged the mare's head around, and reined in.

'This looks pretty good right here,' he muttered. 'A little bit of a windbreak, some screwbean mesquite and a patch of grass for the horses to forage on.'

He swung down from the saddle wearily, stripped the gear and packs off the horses, led the animals to water, then staked them in the galleta grass where they could graze and roll all night.

'Do you cook?' he asked Dolores from the far side of the well.

'I've never had to,' she replied softly, 'but I'm willing to learn.'

He bobbed his head and started digging the battered Dutch oven out of his possibles sack. 'Glad to hear that,' he said. 'For a while there I thought I'd have to do it all.'

She lifted her chin defiantly. 'I may have led a sheltered life, Ned, but I'm not afraid to get my hands dirty.'

'First thing we're going to need is some firewood. Anything that looks like it'll burn.'

A twinge of dismay touched her face for an instant, but she pushed herself up from the slab of rock she was sitting on and met his eyes.

'I'll see what I can find.'

When she had wandered away, Ned settled the packs and saddles in the spot he'd selected, poured a coffee pot full of water into the kettle, and rearranged a few rocks to shelter the fire from the night wind.

Shadows were lengthening and he could already feel the chill of the desert night coming on.

He accepted the wood from Dolores when she stepped back into camp, thumbstruck one of his new-fangled lucifer matches, and had a small fire going in a matter of minutes.

'I brought a few vegetables from town,' he said, handing her a bone-handled Bowie knife, 'and I want to use them up before they spoil in the heat.'

31

He set a few potatoes and carrots on a flat rock next to the fire and nodded toward them. 'If you really want to help, you can start chopping these up and dropping them in the kettle. Just don't cut yourself while you're about it. There's not many doctors around out here and I'm no hand at healing.'

Without another word he started adding pieces of venison jerky into the smoke-blackened Dutch oven and stirred it with a long-handled wooden spoon.

Dolores dropped the last of the vegetables into the pot, adjusted her skirt behind her, and lowered herself to the same slab of rock she'd sat on earlier.

'This stew won't take too long,' he said. 'Half an hour or so.'

'Would you like to hear the real history of the treasure ship while we wait?' she asked in a hushed voice.

He shrugged, knowing in advance she was going to tell him the story whether he wanted to hear it or not.

She was that kind of woman.

'Some time in the early 1600s,' she began, 'a contract was signed between the King of Spain and the Cardona family for them to engage in naval exploration and pearl hunting for the Crown.

'They built three ships in Acapulco and headed out after some delay. From what I've learned, one of the Cardona boys, another man named Juan de Iturbe, and a Sergeant Rosales were the captains.'

'I'd never heard those other names,' Ned said quietly, feeding a mesquite branch into the fire.

He was starting to smell the teasing smell of the stew – a welcome relief from the heady aroma of the creosote. He lifted the lid off the dented Dutch oven and gave the thickening stew another quick stir.

'This Captain Cardona,' Dolores continued, 'was wounded by hostile Indians . . . Seri, I think . . . and went back to Acapulco, but de Iturbe and Rosales continued on to the north and did very well, trading wormy ship's biscuits for pearls with the Indians.

'Apparently the Indians thought the worms made it a good trade.' She smiled at him in the gathering darkness and added, 'I suppose there's just no accounting for taste.'

Ned snorted at her statement. That had been one of his mother's favorite sayings.

'Go on with the story.'

Dolores stared into the fire as if she were mesmerized by the flames and went on, her voice soft and reedy like an Apache flute.

'The story gets a little vague as to what happened to Rosales after that, but it's told that de Iturbe continued on up the Sea of Cortez looking for—'

She stopped abruptly as a muted, ghostly sound came to them from the thicket. Her breath quickened, caught in her throat, and the look of sudden panic that crossed her face told Ned she'd never spent a night in the desert.

'Wha—?'

He held a hand up to stop her and gave a slow shake of his head. 'It's just a screech owl calling for a mate, miss. Nothing to get rattled about.'

Her face colored slightly. She straightened her back and drew an unsteady breath.

'I'm sorry. I . . .'

'De Iturbe continued on up the Sea of Cortez?' he prodded.

She sat facing him with her knees locked together and the slowly strengthening night wind whipped at a few careless curls on the back of her neck.

'Yes,' she said after a moment. 'They say he spotted a vast inland sea and thought he'd found the Strait of Anian, which was supposed to be a passage between the Atlantic and Pacific Oceans, and sailed on up into it to explore. It turned out he was actually in a lake at a time when the Colorado River had overflowed its banks.'

'I could have told you that,' he muttered.

She shrugged. 'Apparently he sailed around in there for a couple of months, looking for the Strait and, when he couldn't find it, headed back south only to find that the passage he'd come in on had dried up behind him.

'The story is that he abandoned his ship, with a vast treasure of black pearls still on board, and he and his crew counted themselves lucky just to get out of there alive.'

The fire crackled quietly, sending a few sparks into the night sky, and Ned considered the information she was handing out – not all that different from the old treasure-ship legend, really. He tucked it away in the back yard of his mind.

Still he didn't pass on the white bird story he'd

been told by the old Cahuilla warrior.

Somehow the time just didn't seem right.

Manny Barajas stood straddle-legged, arms folded across his chest, waiting for the half-breed to walk his horse across to the picket line they'd set up and bring him some news.

'They stopped at the well we heard about in the cantina, Manny,' the tracker mumbled finally.

He stepped down from the pinto he rode, glanced longingly at their small fire, and slapped the dust off his trousers.

'How far ahead?'

Indio cocked his head and stepped a little closer to the fire. 'Maybe an hour.'

'Did they see you?'

'No, I rode slow and raised no dust.'

'Good. Get some food and a good night's sleep,' Barajas said, sweeping his hand toward the fire. 'I'll want you on them again first thing in the morning.'

'I could use a shot of mezcal to cut the dust,' Indio muttered.

'It's there on the rock.'

Manny lowered himself to a chunk of grey sandstone and watched Indio ladle up a plateful of beans and rice from the kettle, resting his chin in the palm of his hand.

'I hate dry camps,' he said idly. 'The horses will be balky tomorrow after getting only a little water from the canteens and there's not much for them to graze on.'

'They'll survive,' Indio said. He spilled another scoop of beans on to a hot tortilla and started wolfing it down.

'And so will we, but I can think of better ways to spend a night.'

The sun dropped behind the mountains far to the west in a blaze of dust-hazy orange. It was only minutes before the night hunters of the desert started making themselves known: the rustling of dry leaves close around them, the haunting call of burrowing owls, and the far off yelps of a prowling coyote.

It was always so in the desert.

Manny scanned their campsite with a jaundiced eye. He knew their fire couldn't be seen from a hundred yards in any direction yet still he didn't feel safe here. It was just too exposed.

He lifted his gaze across the fire to Diego Reyes, the young *pistolero* from Guerrero, and spoke loud enough for all his men to hear.

'I don't trust this place and I want a guard set tonight. Diego, you take the first shift and wake Pepe about midnight.'

They ate in silence when Ned was satisfied the stew was done and he tried to picture Dolores seated at some huge dining table on her ranch in Jalisco, rather than sitting on a slab of rock out here in the middle of the Yuha badlands.

It was an easy image to conjure up.

For himself, he'd spent most of his life in the

36

desert and one more night camped among the sage and mesquite was nothing new to him.

Truth be known, he felt more comfortable in the open than he did with a roof over his head. Somehow, knowing what was around him eased his mind.

He rinsed off the dishes when they were finished eating, set them on the heavy pack, and started thinking about sleep.

It was well known in the West that mustangs were more alert than domestic horses, more aware of their surroundings, and a knowing man took advantage of that, spreading his bedroll near them in the sure knowledge that they would wake him if any kind of danger approached during the night.

Ned Gamble was definitely a knowing man.

CHAPTER FOUR

Ned spread his blanket in the mesquite thicket, not too far from the grulla, using the worn saddle as a pillow, and cradling the heavy Peacemaker in his lap.

He watched silently as Dolores followed suit. She turned her back on him, tugged the blanket up over her shoulders, and snuggled into the sand and gravel as best she could. It would be, he decided, a far cry from the soft feather bed she was used to at home.

The fire would gutter out in an hour or so and he didn't really care. He wanted to save what wood they had for warming up a pot of coffee in the morning.

It would be a small enough blessing.

He lounged back against the saddle and clamped his teeth hard together, thinking morosely about the past and how he'd become what he was.

Most of the men he knew had drifted west at the end of the war, either having nothing left to go home to or looking for a better life, and that just wasn't true of Ned Gamble.

He had been born and raised in the desert country and in reality that was all he'd ever known.

His father had been a well-respected freighter on the Santa Fe Trail for many years, operating a large string of wagons from a freight yard just off the main plaza in Santa Fe. He'd built himself the reputation of being a canny yet scrupulously honest man, and Ned had grown up in his shadow.

He'd started driving for his pa at the ripe old age of twelve, a cumbersome freight wagon with four head of oxen and a hard board seat, making the entire 900-mile journey from Santa Fe to Arrow Rock as well as any man among them.

He'd hunted mule deer and elk in the ragged ridges of the Sangre de Cristo Mountains, northeast of Santa Fe, and had been across the *Jornada del Muerto* dozens of times before he was old enough to shave.

And, even young as he was, he had recognized that the coming of the Atchison, Topeka and Santa Fe Railroad would mark the end of traffic on the trail.

His father died of cholera the year before the railroad crossed the Kaw River, back up in Kansas, and there was little enough to keep him in Santa Fe.

Selling off the wagons and stock didn't bring in as much as it should have and he gave what it did over to his mother. She had little enough to tide her through the rough times that were ahead and Ned could make it on his own.

He drifted west after that – Socorro, Tucson, Gila

Bend – finally signing on to drive for Wells Fargo. After that life became a jumble of occupations.

There was just no one occupation that suited him.

He'd found that he had some kind of strange wanderlust in his soul, always wanting to see what lay beyond that next range of hills, what it was like on the other side of the playa, and it drove him into country that white men had never seen.

A desert rat they called him, and he guessed he deserved the label.

He was at home in the desert, knowing its secret ways, the tricks it played on the reckless, and he never allowed himself to be complacent out there.

The desert did not forgive foolishness.

Ever.

Then the grulla snorted softly in the darkness, shaking her bridle, and Ned sat up, suddenly on edge in the midst of the mesquite thicket.

He glanced around at the mare, to see which way her ears were pointed, and saw instead the figure of a man – a dark shadow, really – crouching down to pull a picket pin.

Without a second's hesitation he lifted the Peacemaker from his lap and pulled the trigger. The shot would have taken the man high in the ribs, just below the armpit if he'd hit what he'd aimed at, and at that distance it would have been hard to miss.

The sudden roar of the shot reverberated through the thicket, silencing the normal night-time sounds of the desert, and every creature out there was instantly alert.

The man he'd shot toppled heavily to the side, his legs twitching in death throes, and, from the corner of his eye, Ned spotted the dark silhouette of another man lunging toward him with some kind of massive war club raised above his head.

He swung the Colt only slightly and squeezed off another round. The man withered to his knees only a few feet away, then pitched forward on his face. The war club battered noisily into the brush.

The loud crack of another shot shattered the night, and Ned felt a bullet tug at his shirt where it bloused out at the waist at the exact same instant as he saw the muzzle flash.

He moved slightly to his left, swung the Peacemaker up, and fired again. From the gurgling wail that followed he figured he must have hit the man in the throat.

The dying man's wail was drowned out a moment later by the thundering beat of horses' hoofs galloping away to the north. Ned pushed himself erect, knowing full well the raid was over.

'Ned?' came Dolores' quaking voice in the darkness.

'I'm here,' he mumbled. 'Can you bring a torch from the fire so we can see what we're up against?'

He exhaled heavily, staring after the horses and letting the significance of the raid soak in.

Without horses they were suddenly in a very bad way.

Quietly he paced across to the first body and nodded for Dolores to hold the torch a little lower.

The man was obviously Indian, wearing nothing but a loose cotton shirt and a loincloth, but his moccasins were unfamiliar.

He reached down with the barrel of the Peacemaker, hooked the front sight in the warrior's shirt, and turned the body over. The man's hair slid slowly to the side and, in the flickering light of the torch, Ned could see the wide lines and dots of an intricate facial tattoo done in blue cactus ink.

'Mojave,' he said, rubbing his hand across the stubble of his beard. 'I should have known. They're one of very few tribes in the country who have no compunction about fighting at night.'

'I don't understand,' Dolores whispered behind him.

'Most Indians don't want to fight at night,' he offered. 'They believe if they're killed at night the Gods can't see them and their spirit will wander in darkness for ever.'

She wagged her head in the scant light of the torch. 'Why didn't they just kill us in our sleep?'

He snorted softly. 'They weren't after us. They were after our horses, and I have to get them back. Without horses we could very easily die out here.'

'It's too dark to track them now,' she moaned and he could almost feel the fear trembling her voice.

'I don't have to track them. I know where they're going. There are only two water holes anywhere near here. San Sebastian Marsh, at the north end of California's Superstition Mountains, and Fish Creek, maybe six miles west of that. If they're not at one, they'll be at the other.'

'How far is it?'

He shrugged. 'Thirty miles give or take. A good ten-hour walk any way you slice it.'

'But it will be morning before you get there,' she whined.

'I know,' he said, 'but it's got to be done. You're here next to water and there's food in the pack, so you should be OK. If I don't make it. . . .'

'What do you mean, if you don't make it?'

'What do you think I mean?' he asked flatly. There was a touch of anger in his voice and he could feel the sensation of it surging through him.

Was the woman so naïve that she didn't recognize that he was flirting with death just by going out there? Had her life been so complacent that she couldn't face reality? Or was it that she just didn't want to try?

'If I don't make it,' he repeated a little more forcefully, 'you persuade some travelers on the trail to take you to Yuma. You'll be all right once you get back there.'

He turned, picking the Big Dipper out of the night sky, traced the imaginary line through the pointers, and located the bright North Star.

That would be his guide, his mark. At least until he reached the Superstitions. There would be time enough to veer off to the left after that.

'Keep the fire going as best you can,' he said. 'It doesn't have to be big, just enough to give you light and a little warmth.'

'You're leaving me out here alone?' she whimpered.

'It can't be helped. It's either this or take our chances on dying.'

He paced away into the darkness, not giving her a chance to rebut his words, and he had no regrets about it.

It was a dog-eat-dog world out here, sweetheart, and he had bigger teeth.

He paused fifty yards out, letting his eyes become better adjusted to the dark, picked out the North Star again, and started forward.

The desert has a different feel at night. As the sun slips down, taking the heat of the day with it, the animals awaken one by one and the desert comes to life.

It is black and white and empty in the early hours of the morning, but there is life out there, and sound.

A gentle wind rustles the leaves and dies away. Then comes yet another rustling sound – a wood rat or jackrabbit easing from one clump of grass to the next – and it, too, fades into the night.

The trail becomes indistinct in the darkness and it is only by focusing on some object in the far distance that a reasonably straight course can be maintained. His distant object was that one bright star hanging low in the northern sky.

He wasn't used to walking – no horseman is – but he did it. Putting one foot in front of the other without really thinking about it, and it felt as if he was making good time.

He was cold and tired but kept moving in spite of it. Clumps of mesquite fingered his clothes, he stumbled once in a while, glanced up at the star every few minutes, and kept doggedly on the trail.

There was no quit in him and never had been.

The angry buzz of a hunting rattlesnake stopped him dead in his tracks after several hours and he stood for a long minute scanning what he could see of the desert in the pale light of the stars.

Mesquite thickets and clumps of crucifixion thorn stood like islands of darkness amid the low mud hills and he could barely make out the mound of the Superstitions still several miles off to the north.

It would be light in a couple more hours, and he still had a long way to go.

The whir of the offended rattler tapered off as the reptile slithered away into the darkness, and Ned plucked a few mesquite leaves he could chew on to stave off his thirst.

With a stubbornness born of necessity he forced himself to move on.

He'd been to San Sebastian Marsh before, on his first trip to the coast. As a matter of fact, he recalled, that was where he'd met old Huarache.

It was a low swampy area at the junction of San Felipe and Carrizo Creeks, the site of a prehistoric Indian village, and was as likely a spot for pitching camp as anyone was going to find out here. There was always plenty of water, salt grass for the horses, and an ironwood thicket for firewood.

Animals frequented the area to slake their thirst and a patient man could always bring down some camp meat.

He knew, from talk around the campfires at night, that de Anza had named the place for Sebastian Tarabal, a Cochimi Indian from Baja California who had guided him on both of his overland expeditions to the coast.

It was a fitting enough tribute to the man, he supposed, but he could hardly have been considered a saint.

Still, Ned had no idea what he'd find at the marsh.

If he found anything at all.

It would be just like the Mojaves to water the horses, let them forage a little, and move on to their home territory, eager to show off the booty they'd taken in their raids against the Kumeyaay tribe farther to the south and now on the white-eyes at Yuha Well.

Mile after mile fell behind him as he staggered, falling to his knees now and again and using the saddle rifle to push himself back up from the grittiness of the sand.

Suddenly the Superstitions were there, pushing up into the early morning sky on his right. He smelled wood smoke and roasting meat and halted again, to look, to listen, to feel.

Peering through the scattered brush and rocks he saw the edge of the marsh, the arrow weed and creosote bushes, the stands of bulrush beckoning from the dark water. He caught the flickering glow of a small fire through the thicket and edged silently closer.

A mule deer lifted his head from one of the many springs and watched him, silvered droplets of water falling away from his muzzle, but he didn't run.

A few more steps then and the Mojave camp came magically into view.

Ned stepped into the darkness that remained under a grizzled ironwood tree and studied the layout for several minutes.

The horses he'd come after were not in sight – possibly they were in the stand of mesquite beyond the camp – but everything else was right there in front of him.

A lone warrior, nearly naked, sat cross-legged before the fire, roasting what appeared to be a jackrabbit carcass on a long stick. Beyond him, another warrior sat on a bed of matted grass, finger-combing his long hair and chanting something that sounded suspiciously like the old Navajo twelve-word Blessingway Song.

Ned counted four others, still asleep, beyond these two and everything seemed peaceful in their world.

At least until he stepped away from the tree.

The Peacemaker was already drawn, hanging heavily in his work-hardened hand, and he was in no mood for conversation.

The warrior at the fire spotted him first and let out a yapping, coyote-like war cry, 'Yai, yai, yai, yai. . . .'

One of the men he'd thought was asleep rolled up on his side and fired his pistol three times in rapid succession.

His shots were all high and to the right.

Ned's weren't.

He swung the long-barreled Peacemaker up, squeezed off two rounds, and blew the man back over on to his bedding.

An arrow hissed by his head at that instant and he turned only slightly, singled out a tall warrior holding a bow, and fired again.

The bullet took the man in the chest, flung him backwards a pace or two into a clump of brittle arrow weed, where he lay still.

He swung next to the warrior at the fire, just then getting to his feet, and dropped him with a single shot to the head.

The Blessingway chanter was next.

The slender warrior lifted what appeared to be a Spencer repeating carbine left over from the Civil War, fired once and was working the lever to load a fresh cartridge into the chamber when Ned's shot took him in the cheek.

He too was jerked a pace backwards, landing close to the warrior who'd fired the arrow a moment earlier.

Ned felt rather than saw another man leaping towards him, and slashing downward with a wicked stone-headed war club. Ned dropped to one knee, brought the Peacemaker up, and fired almost point blank into the man's chest.

The warrior clawed at Ned's face and shirt as he went down, his elaborate facial tattoo suddenly smeared red with the blood spilling from his nose and mouth.

A young-looking Mojave on the far side of the camp rose to his feet then, sprinting away to the north, toward the mesquite thicket where Ned thought the horses might be. There was no time to reload.

He dropped the Colt to the gravel, lifted the saddle rifle he'd lugged all night, and drilled the stripling through the back.

The young warrior's arms flailed wildly in the pale light of dawn; he took another few running strides, and went down face first in a deep patch of salt grass.

Another rifle shot shattered the morning, and Ned felt the astonishing burn as the bullet creased the side of his neck.

He jacked a new round into the Winchester's chamber, turned slightly, and blew the last Mojave he could see off his feet.

Nothing else moved and slowly . . . very slowly . . . Ned let himself relax.

He lowered himself to one knee, still peering into the ironwood thicket, retrieved the Peacemaker from the gravel, and slid it back into his holster.

The silence that settled over San Sebastian Marsh after the crashing thunder of the gunshots was almost unbelievable.

Mourning doves began their calling a few minutes after the shooting ended and it wasn't long before they had drowned out all other sound in the marsh.

The eastern horizon turned gradually lighter and the heavy grey shadows of the early desert morning began taking on their more familiar shapes of brush and cactus and rock.

Ned exhaled heavily, staggered on to the fire, and glanced tiredly at the bodies strewn around him.

He'd been lucky, there was no doubt in his mind about that, for these were fighting men, schooled in one of the harshest environments on the face of the earth. To them warfare was not something you stumbled into once in a while and scratched your way out of if you were able. To them it was a way of life.

And they were damned good at it.

He uncapped his canteen and drank deeply. It had been a long night and he still had the day ahead of him.

Touching the side of his neck, he bobbed his head dubiously when his hand came away bloody. He reached back up with his ragged blue bandanna, hoping against hope that putting pressure on the wound would stem the flow of blood.

He really had been lucky, he decided. Another inch and the shot would have clipped his jugular vein, and there would have been precious little he could do about it.

Without the slightest twinge of remorse he lifted the long roasting-stick out of the fire and sank his teeth into the hind leg of the crisply cooked jackrabbit skewered on it.

What the hell, he mused, the Mojave warriors

he'd just sent to their happy hunting ground were not going to miss it.

He chewed slowly, savoring the gamey taste of the rabbit, gazing away at the Fish Creek Mountains, maybe six miles west of the Superstitions.

From this distance few peaks were visible, but he knew from past trips that it was a land of jagged ridges and deep, rock-ribbed canyons, where there was almost always water in shallow tanks.

On the lower slopes a man had to dodge agave spears and the spines of teddy-bear cholla, but a little higher up the ridges were covered with stands of juniper, pinyon pine, and scattered pools of water surrounded by swaying fan palms.

It meant shade and cool breezes coming down from the peaks, a chance to get off your feet for a while, nurse a cup of hot, black coffee, and work the kinks out of your back.

He had a long ride ahead of him, back to Yuha Well for the Torreón woman and his gear, and another long ride to the Fish Creeks after that, but that would be the place for their camp tonight.

San Sebastian Marsh, with dead bodies bloated by the heat of the day, was out of the question.

CHAPTER FIVE

'What the hell are you doing back?' Barajas blurted at the half-breed when he rode into camp. 'I told you to watch them.'

'Nothing to worry about, Manny. There's been a change.'

'Change?'

Indio lifted his hands dubiously. 'Looks like they got hit by Indians last night. The horses are gone and so is the gringo. Three dead bodies lying around with vultures and coyotes picking them apart. They made so damned much commotion I could get in real close without being seen or heard.'

'And?'

'Dolores was sitting in the brush quite a way from their campsite and hiding her eyes from all the scavenging.'

'Three bodies?' Manny asked, wide-eyed. 'That means this gringo really *is* a fighter like we were told. What happened to him?'

'No idea,' the half-breed answered with a shrug.

'He wasn't one of the dead guys. The horse tracks were headed north but the soil is so hard I couldn't see any boot prints. Either he took the horses and left her out there on her own or the Indians carried him off. Either way we got plenty of time.'

Barajas pressed his thin lips together and narrowed his eyes. 'Damn. I hadn't expected anything like that.'

'I don't think the gringo did, either,' Indio replied.

Manny turned away, peering at the barren, grey flats, which stretched for miles in every direction.

'We need to know what happened to the gringo, Indio, and we need to know soon.' He stroked his mustache for a moment and went on:

'I want you to go back out there,' he droned. 'Follow the horses' tracks, wherever they went, and find out what happened to this Gamble character. Without him, we've got no reason to be here.'

'Damn, Manny,' Indio complained, 'they could have gone to kingdom come for all I know. This could take days.'

'And we don't have days. Take whatever food and water you think you'll need, but I want you to head back out. You're the only tracker I've got.'

'Any of that mezcal left?'

'Yeah, just don't get yourself drunk,' Manny said evenly. 'I need you at your best.'

Indio shrugged his narrow shoulders and looked away. 'Yeah, yeah, whatever you say.'

The half-breed paced away toward the fire,

tucking his shirt into his trousers a little better, and Manny watched him go.

His mind drifted back to the comfort of Acapulco for a moment, to his family and friends, to everything they'd left behind to ride up here.

His father was a fisherman, earning his living from the sea, and Manny had grown up in the *barrio* of Icacos, east of town, where many of the fishermen lived.

There was always plenty of dorado and mackerel to eat, of course, sometimes even the succulent red *calamares*, and, if his father had had a very good day on the water, he could sell part of his catch in the market. Then there would be a little money in the house for corn and rice and beans.

That always made his mother happy.

But Icacos was a tough little *barrio* and boys learned to fight with their fists at an early age. They all knew each other but that mattered very little.

Either you could handle yourself or you couldn't.

If you couldn't, you got your ass handed to you every couple of days whether you liked it or not. He smiled grimly, remembering it.

Because of his size, he'd never been able to put up much of a fight and he'd had to figure out a different way to survive.

The one thing he found he had over the other boys in the *barrio* was a way with words.

He could tell a believable lie with a straight face, turn the other kids into rivals, and set them up to take out their anger on each other instead of on him.

Over the years he'd managed to work himself into a position of leadership, where the other boys came to him for ideas and guidance.

He had always been able to tell them how to earn a quick peso, which stalls in the market had goods that could be lifted, and which girls in the *barrio* were tumbling.

That was exactly how this little band had been formed: by planting the idea that there would be riches in store for any man who rode with him.

Five old friends from the *barrio* and Indio, the half-breed Yaqui from somewhere high in the Sierra Madre Mountains.

It was more than enough, that much he was sure of.

Yet he had no intention of becoming a fisherman like his father.

No, sir.

What he wanted was land.

A big rancho in the hills above Icacos where white-faced cattle could graze and get fat, where he could build a sprawling hacienda and establish himself as head of the family.

Don Miguel Barajas, he mused.

It almost rolled off the tongue.

He had learned of the pearls almost by accident.

A friend of his father, living in Acapulco, had been approached a few years ago by the Torreóns about buying some of them. The price had been exceedingly low, indicating that they hoped for a quick sale.

After that Manny had made a point of being seen in the town of San Sebastián del Oeste, where the Torreóns lived, riding a beautiful palomino stallion to attract attention to himself.

He'd struck up an acquaintance with Dolores after mass one Sunday morning and very gradually wound his way into her plan to search for the pearls.

As a matter of fact, it was he who had recommended Ned Gamble as a guide. A few letters to his cousin, working in a cantina in Nogales, had given him the gringo's name and told of his hard-earned reputation.

It had been up to Dolores to persuade him to take the job, but that was something she could accomplish with no problems.

She had a way with men.

Now they were here; camped in a shallow bowl in the middle of nowhere, desolation all around, and no way of telling how much longer it would last.

He needed time to think.

Ned finished eating the roasted rabbit, washing it down with long drinks from his canteen, and sat quietly beside the sputtering fire for a few minutes, feeding new rounds into the six-shooter and rifle.

It was a foolish man who carried an empty weapon in this part of the world.

And he didn't count himself among them.

At last he pushed himself to his feet, paced on into the mesquite thicket and found the stolen horses right where he'd thought they'd be.

He gathered the reins of his three, led them to water, refilled his canteen, then came back and slipped the hackamores off the Indian ponies. He shied them away with his sweat-stained hat and stood silently, watching them lope away to the north.

Like all horses, they would be home-bodies. Chances were they'd simply drift back to wherever they'd been captured in the first place and live out their lives in an area they were familiar with.

He grabbed a handful of mane, vaulted up on to the grulla's back, and tugged her head around toward Yuha Well.

The first dust-hazy rays of dawn were peeking over the rounded knolls of the Superstitions, warming away the early-morning chill, and the night hunters began retreating into their cool burrows and crevices for shelter from the coming heat.

He tugged the brim of his hat a little lower over his eyes against the building brilliance of the day and studied the flat horizon ahead of him.

Nothing out of the ordinary met his eye, nothing but the burned out hills and scraggy desert brush.

That was just the way he liked it.

Ned heeled the mare into a shambling trot back along the trail and settled into the smooth motion of the mountain-bred grulla's gait.

The sun climbed steadily into the brassy summer sky, heat waves shimmered and danced around him, and he felt the weariness from lack of sleep creeping into his bones.

The grulla's ears perked suddenly forward as they

rode and she looked off to the left as though she might have smelled another horse.

Ned let her slow to a standstill on the pretext of wiping the sweatband of his hat, but his eyes were busy searching the creosote and clumps of mesquite well off the trail.

Too many years of surviving in Chiricahua country had taught him a very valuable lesson: just because you can't see anyone out there doesn't mean you're alone.

He'd seen Apaches bury themselves in the sand so that the only things left uncovered were their nostrils, then rise up, seeming to come from nowhere, and ambush a group of passing riders.

Hiding a horse would not be as easy, but he had no doubt it could be done. A shallow bowl in the flats would be all it took.

He had no doubt that, if anyone could do it, it would be an Indian.

He spent several minutes studying the brush-covered flats to the left of the trail, the likely hiding-spots, the places an Indian would force his mount to lie down in, but nothing grabbed his attention.

Not wanting to be too obvious about it, he nudged the mare into a slow walk after a few more moments, but he had a strange sensation between his shoulder blades that a rifle was being sighted in on him at that very moment.

Some man he didn't even know was waiting patiently to gun him down.

He rode cautiously after that, putting distance behind him, but found himself glancing over his shoulder time and again, checking for dust on his back trail.

He didn't like the feeling.

Dolores cowered in the scant shade of the mesquite thicket fifty yards west of the well and it was only the stark whiteness of her blouse that gave away her position.

He spotted her from a quarter of a mile out, rode directly up to her, and reined in a few feet away, not understanding why she was this far from their camp.

'What are you doing way over here?' he asked with a frown.

She jerked her head toward the well and grimaced. 'I wanted to be as far away from them as I could possibly get.'

'Them?'

'The bodies you left behind,' she said irritably. 'It was horrible. The birds showed up first, picking at their faces and the bullet holes in them, hissing at the other birds. Then the coyotes came and drove the birds away. They've been trotting back and forth all morning, carrying bits of flesh off into the desert.'

She tipped her head back then, peering at the cloudless sky above them, at the dozens of dark turkey vultures circling over their heads.

'Look at them,' she groused. 'Still up there. Just waiting for a chance to come down.'

'I got the horses back,' he ventured, wanting to

change the subject.

'Good. Can we leave this place?'

'You want to eat something first?'

She huffed loudly at his question and pushed herself to her feet. 'I don't think I could.'

'Suit yourself. I'll get the horses saddled up and we'll make tracks out of here.'

He dropped off the grulla's back, ground-hitched the three horses where they could reach water, shoved the Dutch oven back into his possibles sack, and started throwing the saddles and packs on the horses almost by rote.

It would be much the same at San Sebastian Marsh with the vultures and coyotes, he was reasonably sure of that, and he nodded at his thought to avoid that area altogether tonight.

He splashed his face and chest with water, stepped into the saddle, and walked the horses back to where Dolores waited.

She needed help climbing into the saddle again, but it was only a matter of minutes before they were trailing north out of Yuha Well.

They rode silently through a stretch of mud hills strewn with sparkling chips of gypsum crystal, through the patches of brittle bursage, mesquite, and creosote, eventually veering off the wagon road toward the sawtooth ridges of the San Jacinto range.

He remembered a narrow box canyon in the foothills up there where sweet, cold water burbled down over smooth blueish rocks, stately fan palms and scrub oaks provided shade on even the brightest of days. The steep canyon walls would reflect the heat of their fire at night and they could not be approached except through the mouth of the narrow cleft.

It would at least guarantee him a good night's sleep and a place to cook a meal that stuck to a man's ribs.

They'd be in Cahuilla country then. The tribe had lived in that area for thousands of years, was known to be peaceful, and controlled the mountain passes.

Ned knew they traded with the Mojaves to the east, corn and beans for shell beads from the coast, but there was no love lost between the two tribes.

The Cahuilla knew him from previous trips through their country, knew he had no base designs on them or their land, and counted him as a friend.

In country like the desolate Yuha badlands it was a very good thing to have friends.

'You get any sleep last night?' he asked over his shoulder.

'No,' she said wearily. 'I was too afraid to fall asleep.'

He exhaled heavily and wagged his head in disbelief. 'You should have stayed home, lady. I've said it before and I'll say it again . . . you don't belong out here.'

'If I had stayed home, Mr Gamble,' she said defiantly, 'I would eventually not have had a home.'

She rode in silence after that, stiff-necked and refusing to look at him, twirling her flimsy French parasol above her head like a character clown in

Barnum and Bailey's traveling circus.

She was thoroughly miffed at him, and he just didn't care.

He was right and he knew it.

CHAPTER SIX

Indio waited several minutes after the gringo he'd been trailing and the woman rode out of Yuha Well before he got off the horse's neck and stood up.

The vultures had wasted no time in descending again after they'd left, flapping their great wings at each other and strutting around the bodies.

He peered north along the trail, watching Dolores and the gringo disappear into the distance before he moved. Even then it was only to tug the pinto to its hoofs.

It had been a part of his Yaqui upbringing to be overly cautious in all things, weighing the good against the bad, and that training had stayed with him his entire life.

He led the horse south for a quarter of a mile before he climbed into the saddle, then rode slowly so that he raised no telltale dust plume. He worked his way back through the scattered stands of mesquite that covered the Yuha plains and finally dropped down into the shallow bowl where Manny had chosen to pitch camp. Every man there was waiting for his report, and he knew it.

He stepped down from the saddle on the far side of the fire and took a quick swig of warm mezcal before turning toward Barajas.

'He's still alive, Manny,' he said, wiping his mouth on his shirtsleeve.

'You saw him?'

'Damn sure did. I swung wide of the well and followed the horse tracks north like you said. An hour or so up the trail I spotted a dust ahead of me, rode way the hell and gone back into the brush, and forced the horse down.'

He took another swallow of the fiery mezcal, caught his breath, and continued:

'I think the gringo suspected something right about there, though, 'cause he stopped and looked the area over pretty good. Didn't pick me out but I'd guess he's riding all keyed up right about now.'

Barajas cocked his head. 'You sure he didn't spot you?'

'Certain sure. I trailed him back to the well and watched while he saddled up, then him and the woman headed back north.'

'Well,' Manny said grinning. 'I guess we still have a reason to be out here.'

He turned to the rest of the men and smiled grimly. 'Saddle up, *muchachos.* It's time to ride.'

The shadow of the high hills west of them was steadily pushing out on to the desert floor and Ned could already feel the chill evening wind leaking down the slopes.

The landmarks here were subtle compared to those in the Arizona Territory, but he was eventually able to pick out the dark cut that marked the entrance to the slot canyon that he remembered.

He guided the horses carefully past the rubble of boulders that clogged the entrance and walked them slowly in through the narrow cleft.

Fifty yards in, past a pile of smoke-blackened boulders, he turned into another pinched canyon that opened suddenly on to a wide, hushed bowl hidden behind the massive, ancient cliffs.

Tall shade trees reached skyward between the steep rock walls and wind-blown sand muffled all sound.

As he remembered, the creek tumbled quietly over worn blue-grey rocks, emptying into a deep pool of clear mountain water. A thick stand of galleta grass and screwbean mesquite backed up to the slopes and was a perfect place for the horses to graze.

The soft rustling of leaves overhead, the burbling of water in the pool, and the occasional call of a camp-robber jay were the only sounds that disturbed the hush of the place. Ned heaved a great sigh of relief that he'd been able to find it again.

He swung down from the saddle, led the horses to the edge of the pool, and helped Dolores down from her perch.

'We'll be safe here,' he told her. 'It's a good place

to recuperate and get the horses back in shape.'

'I'm tired,' she said with a sigh.

'So am I,' he agreed, 'but we've still got things to do. If you want to gather some firewood while we've still got light, I'll get a fire going and start something to eat.'

Dolores blew a wayward strand of hair away from her face, collapsed her flimsy parasol, and leaned it against a rock.

'I'll see what I can find.'

'Good,' he said quietly. 'It'll be a while before we eat.'

He paced away into the gathering darkness and quiet of the canyon, stripped the gear off the horses, and staked them out in the grass.

Dolores was just stepping back into their campsite with an armload of firewood when he got back. He grinned at her. 'You ever had hoe cakes?'

'I don't think so,' she answered. 'Is that something you brought away from your great war?'

He huffed at her question. 'I brought a lot of things away from the war, miss.'

Without another word he tented the kindling she'd carried in a circle of rocks that looked as if it had been used as a fire pit many times before, thumbstruck one of his Lucifer matches and got a small, smokeless fire going.

He dipped a coffee pot full of water from the deep pool, started a kettle of bacon and beans, and gazed away into the shadows, pondering her question.

Yes, he *had* brought things away from the war, most of them not so nice, and he remembered every single day of it, every single shot.

He'd ridden down to Fort Craig the day after Governor Connelly put out his call for men and enlisted in the famous First US Cavalry. He was assigned as a scout for Company D of the regiment simply because he was familiar with the area and fought every major battle in New Mexico with them: the defense of Fort Craig, Valverde, Glorietta Pass, Albuquerque, and finally Peralta.

He'd been one of the men who rappelled down the rocky cliff at Glorietta Pass to destroy the Confederate supply train on Tony Johnson's ranch, and that fight had proved to be the high-water mark for the south in New Mexico.

He remembered all too well the ear-shattering echoes of the artillery fire in that rocky canyon, the heaps of dead bodies at the bottom, and the bloodied soldiers who could do no more than drag themselves out of harm's way.

He remembered, too, the glowering face of the so-called Fighting Parson – Major John M. Chivington – who had been hailed as a military hero after the battle of Glorietta Pass and named 'The Butcher of Sand Creek' for his merciless attack on Black Kettle's camp just a little over two years later.

The Cheyenne and Arapaho camped at Sand Creek had flown the American flag over their tepees to show they were friendly, yet Chivington's troops had massacred and mutilated everyone there.

It was said the men in camp, either too old or too young to hunt, were killed out of hand, the women cut to pieces, scalped, their brains knocked out, and little boys had their testicles cut off to be made into tobacco pouches.

The story was the soldiers rode back into Denver wearing women's body parts pinned to their uniforms like badges of honor.

It was enough to give a man pause.

He forced himself back to the reality of the moment and started slicing bacon into the pot of beans.

'That little book of yours,' he mumbled staring at her across the fire, 'what does it say we're looking for?'

'I wondered when you were going to ask that,' Dolores said. 'It's on page thirty-four, and I know it by heart. It says they moored to some rocks in a nearly landlocked cove, protected from the wind and seas, took all their possessions, and abandoned ship.'

He winced at her answer. 'And that's all? I thought you said there was detailed information as to the ship's location in it. There must be half a dozen canyons in these hills that would match that description.'

'Well, at least we know it's in a canyon.'

'Damn,' he blurted, 'that's a lot of territory to cover.'

'Not so much.'

'You know the water could have been a couple hundred feet deep in here at that time, don't you?

That means we've got to search a mile or so back in every canyon we come to.'

She shrugged. 'It could be worse.'

'Really?' he asked incredulously. 'I'll be damned if I know how. We don't have enough food to last us more than a couple of weeks. That means I'll have to take time off from searching for the ship to bring us in some camp meat. Skin it and butcher it and hope it lasts in this heat.'

'Are you always this grouchy?' she asked imperiously.

All he could do was wag his head at her question. 'Are you always this simple-minded?'

The half-breed Yaqui reined in beside the road, waiting for the others to come up to him. When they did, he caught Manny's eyes.

'You see that?' he asked, pointing at the tracks to the left of the trail.

'I see it,' Barajas replied curtly. 'Is there supposed to be something special about horse tracks in sand these days?'

Indio rolled his eyes at Manny's question. 'Believe me, *these* tracks are special. They say the gringo has left the wagon road and headed for the mountains.'

'That's a little strange, isn't it? It's common knowledge there's a marsh north of here and his horses need water as bad as ours do. I thought he was a knowing man.'

The half-breed tilted his head as though he couldn't quite believe Barajas didn't recognize the

69

importance of these tracks.

'He *is* a knowing man, Manny. And these tracks say he knows where there's more water.'

Barajas considered the 'breed's words for a long moment, then looked back up. 'You're the only one I can rely on in this, Indio, the only one who can read scuff marks on the ground. What do you think we should do?'

Indio hunched his shoulders and met the leader's eyes. 'I think you and the boys should stay on the road up to that marsh. Like you said, our horses need water.

'Me, I'm going to follow these tracks and see if I can find out where they camp. If I go with you and the wind picks up tonight I might not be able to cut his tracks again tomorrow and I don't want to chance it.'

'All right, then,' Barajas mumbled. 'You know where we'll be.'

'I'll find you.'

Manny booted his horse in the flanks and started away. 'Let's ride,' he called to the men.

He looked back from a hundred yards up the road and saw the Yaqui, leaning down in the saddle, picking his way through the brush and searching for sign on the hard-packed soil of the flats.

It could not be an easy task and he was a little in awe that anyone at all could manage it.

He'd never been quite sure how Indio had fallen in with his group – a shot of mezcal in a village cantina, if he remembered right – but he was damned glad to have him along.

Truth be known, he knew very little about the man. He had the smooth mannerisms of a pure Mexican and the temperament of a completely wild Yaqui.

One day, Manny decided, there would be a drastic awakening in the man. When one side or the other proved dominant.

If it was the incredibly fierce Yaqui character that came out on top, they could all be in serious trouble.

Another hour brought them to the marsh they'd been told of. Manny saw the swarm of buzzards wheeling low over the ironwood thicket below the hill and knew in advance what it meant.

It would be just as it was at Yuha Well, maybe worse, with dead bodies scattered around, vultures and coyotes feeding on their remains, and he had no desire to camp among all the scavenging.

He spotted the pool of scummy water through the bulrushes and skirted the edge of it until he came to a stream, only a trickle of water, really, that fed clean mountain water into the stagnant marsh.

'This will have to do, boys,' he announced. 'Get the horses watered and a fire going. We may be here for a while.'

He stepped wearily down from the saddle and let his gaze swing to the hazy shelf of mountains off to the west.

This venture, this following Dolores Torreón north from Jalisco, was taking far too long – much longer than he had expected – and he was rapidly getting tired of it.

He was tired of riding, tired of sleeping on the hard ground, tired of eating poorly prepared food, tired of living like a savage in a savage land.

He longed for civilization again, having good friends around him, a noisy cantina on a Saturday night, and the comfort of a willing woman.

Ned finished the last of his bacon and beans, carried the dishes to the quiet pool and rinsed them off in the clear, cold water.

The downslope wind had started as soon as the sun went down and he could see the oak branches above them swaying slightly in the scant light of the fire.

Dolores had dug a long-handled brush out of her *aparejo* and was seated on a dusky fan-palm log in the darker shadows of the canyon, methodically stroking her hair.

He couldn't quite figure her out.

Being feminine in the comfort of some big hacienda deep in the south of Mexico was one thing, ignoring the tasks that had to be done in order to survive in the desert was quite another.

And having to do them all was wearing on him.

'I'll be leaving you alone for a little while,' he told her when he returned to the fire.

'Alone?'

He set the dishes down on the flat surface of a boulder to dry and nodded. 'I won't be long. Just want to have a quick look around.'

'The last time—' she began.

'You're safe enough here,' he said, cutting her off with an upraised hand. He turned on his heel and paced away, not giving her a chance to continue the tirade he knew was coming.

A small game trail, barely visible in the wan light of the stars, led him to the top of the ridge. He eased himself down on a chunk of rock, listening for any odd sound in the desert night and scanning the horizon.

After a moment he spotted a tiny pinpoint of light far off to the east: it could only be a campfire and he squinted his eyes to study it.

It could be anyone, he reflected, but he knew in his heart it wasn't.

No, it was that same group of half a dozen or so riders who had raised the dust behind them coming out of Yuma. The same group that chose not to come in to Yuha Well.

It was strange behavior for anyone traveling this road.

A little too strange to be ignored.

And this, after being watched on the road riding back from the marsh this morning?

He clamped his teeth together and bobbed his head soberly. He had to start being more cautious.

Dolores had already turned in by the time he got back to their encampment and he breathed a sigh of relief at the sight.

A least he wouldn't have to hear more of her belly-aching.

He poured himself another cup of coffee, fed an oak branch into the fire, and sat back to ponder the situation.

The horses were none the worse for being driven so hard by the Mojave raiding party and he was reasonably sure they'd be in fair shape after a night of grazing and rolling.

It was Dolores Torreón who bothered him.

She'd come apart at the seams after the Mojave hit. Having to sit alone in the mesquite thicket, defenseless and unsure of herself, seemed to have taken all the starch out of her and she was rapidly becoming a problem.

Sadly, Ned Gamble had no patience with problems.

CHAPTER SEVEN

Manny Barajas accepted a plate of rice and refried beans from young Diego Reyes, folded a warm corn tortilla in the palm of his hand, and scooped up a mouthful.

He leaned forward, elbows on his knees, and chewed slowly, trying to find some flavor in the food, but felt disgusted by it.

He scanned the members of his small gang, every one of them lounging back against a saddle or rock and gazing into the dancing flames of the fire.

He knew that staring into a campfire was the mark of a real greenhorn – it made it so a man couldn't see well in the dark – but it was a mesmerizing pastime and after a minute he found he was doing it, too.

Reyes shoved another piece of ironwood into the flames with his boot, sending a shower of sparks lifting into the dark night sky. Manny gazed after them as they rose.

He shifted his eyes to the west as there came the

whisking sound of a horse being walked into camp
. . . and found it was true: he really couldn't see well
in the dark. His hand slid to the butt of his pistol in
apprehension, and he waited.

It was Indio coming back from tracking Dolores
and the gringo. He was taking his time about dis-
mounting.

The half-breed ground-hitched his horse, sauntered around the small fire, and fixed young Diego
with tired eyes.

'Anything left to eat?'

'Frijoles and rice, Indio,' Reyes answered quietly.
'Help yourself.'

'How about the mezcal? I've got a powerful thirst
on.'

'There's not much left.'

'What did you find out?' Barajas interrupted.

'They're camped in a canyon in the foothills,'
Indio replied, jerking his head to the west. 'They
didn't have enough firewood for more than one
night, so I'm thinking they'll ride on in the
morning.'

'Farther north?'

Indio shrugged at the question, eyeing the kettle
beside the fire. 'Hard to say. Someone will have to
watch them.'

'I can send Paco or Pepe out in the morning.'

'No,' Indio said with a slow shake of his head.
'This gringo knows the ways of the desert too well.
He'd spot either one of them in a heartbeat.'

'And?'

'I'll go out again. I'm probably the only one who can get away with it.'

'You're sure?' Manny asked, squinting at him.

'Yeah. Let me get some grub in me and a couple hours of sleep and I'll be over there before sunup. I know the ways of the desert, too.'

Barajas nodded his acceptance of the *vaquero*'s words, feeling relieved that he'd volunteered. Still, he didn't like the situation they were in.

'And what of us?'

'You guys just sit tight. I'll ride back and let you know where he is after they pitch camp again.'

'Suit yourself. As for me, I'm getting damned tired of this waiting game.'

'Yeah? Well, this whole thing was your idea, Manny. The rest of us are just along for the ride.'

'Yes,' Manny said flatly, 'it *was* my idea, and if we end up rich as kings because of it, you can all thank me for it.'

Ned awoke to the rich cooing of white-winged doves drowning out the early morning voices of other birds. In the distance he could hear the painful yelps of a lone coyote.

He sat up rolling his head, trying to get the kinks out of his neck. He glanced quickly at the dark canyon around them, and his eyes settled on a slender Indian sitting cross-legged at the embers of their fire, drawing lazily on a long clay pipe.

'I am Lagarto,' the warrior rumbled staring back at him. 'Lizard. And you are the white-eye friend of

77

Huarache.'

'Name's Ned Gamble,' he offered. 'And I do count Huarache as a friend. Is he well?'

'He is well. He is hunting in the mountains north of here. If you want, I can take you to him.'

'I'd appreciate that. I would like to see him again.' He squinted at the Cahuilla brave and tilted his head. 'I seem to remember you.'

Lagarto nodded ponderously and pointed at him with the stem of his pipe. 'Yes, I remember you, too. Four winters ago at Agua Caliente. You rode a Palouse horse and everyone wanted to trade with you.'

Ned smiled at his words, remembering the rump-spotted mare he'd ridden at the time, the distinctive lope she'd had that wasn't quite a canter and wasn't quite a trot. He'd heard a horse trader in Santa Fe once refer to the Palouse's rolling gait as the 'Nez Perce Shuffle' and knew exactly what he meant.

'Yeah,' he said, 'that was a good little horse. She got hit by a stray bullet out in the desert, couldn't stand up any more, and I had to finish her off.'

Lagarto bobbed his head in understanding. 'I always felt bad when I had to do that. A good horse that has carried you far and you have to put a bullet in its brain.'

Ned sloshed the remains of last night's coffee around in the pot and set it next to the fire to heat up.

Dolores sat up, hugging the blanket to her chest,

and eyed the Indian suspiciously.

'This is Lagarto of the Agua Caliente band,' Ned murmured, sweeping his hard hand toward the Cahuilla. 'He's going to lead us on to the north.'

'Good hunting where Huarache is,' Lagarto said evenly. 'Big mule deer and raccoons. Sometimes even bighorn sheep. Plenty of water and forage for the horses, too.'

'Who's Huarache?' Dolores asked quietly.

'An old friend of mine,' Ned answered.

She shrugged as if his words held no importance for her and that irritated him. 'Is there anything to eat?'

'Leftover bacon and beans,' he said. 'I can warm them up.'

He turned back to the Cahuilla warrior and ducked his head toward the kettle. 'How about you, Lagarto? You hungry?'

'I don't care much for bacon and beans.'

Ned huffed at his reply. 'I don't, either,' he muttered, 'but it seems like that's all I've been having for the last couple of years.'

He nudged the smoke-blackened kettle a little closer to the fire, lifted the lid, and gave the beans a quick stir with the long-handled wooden spoon.

'I'll saddle up while they're heating and we can ride out as soon as we're done eating.'

Ned pushed himself erect, ambled away to the horses, and threw the saddles and packs on in a matter of minutes. He led the animals closer to the fire and sat down.

The sun was lifting above the ridges surrounding the canyon and he could feel the building heat in spite of the shade of the cliffs.

Lagarto stuffed his pipe with another pinch of rich coyote tobacco and leaned back, drawing on it slowly, while Ned and Dolores dished up their left-over breakfast.

'You going to the coast?' he asked quietly.

'No,' Ned answered. 'I'm showing her where the padres came through all those years ago.'

The Cahuilla bobbed his head somberly and fixed his button-black eyes on Dolores.

'I have heard the stories,' he said softly. 'Many winters ago. They say the people showed the padres where to find water and what they could eat. They say the people cured their sick and entertained them. And, as a way of thanking them, the padres made them slaves, starved them and tortured them, forced them to live as the white-eyes lived, and many died building their chain of missions.'

'Oh, I don't believe any of that!' Dolores blurted into the silence of the canyon.

'It's true, miss,' Ned countered, 'whether you believe it or not. The Indians had no immunity to the European diseases and hundreds of them died while living at the missions. Anyway, enough of this. Let's get some breakfast in us and get started.'

They ate quickly and in silence, Lagarto reading the look on Dolores' face and wagging his head at her reaction.

Ned, too, had been a little surprised at her outburst.

It was one thing to be angered by the injustices of the past, he thought, but quite another to deny them altogether.

Without a word he collected their dirty dishes, rinsed them off in the pool, and shoved them once again into his possibles sack.

He kicked sand and gravel over what remained of their fire and led the big sorrel mare to a rock where Dolores could climb into the saddle without his help.

'It is good you take care of her, Ned Gamble,' Lagarto said close to his shoulder. 'She would never survive out here on her own.'

Ned nodded his agreement without speaking, climbed into the saddle, and nudged the grulla into a slow walk toward the mouth of the canyon.

'You know you're being watched, don't you?' Lagarto asked across the narrow space between their mounts.

Ned bobbed his head once and cut his eyes away toward the flats. 'I'm thinking it's an Indian from across the river,' he replied. 'I've been seeing dust behind us ever since we left Yuma.'

'I picked up his sign this morning,' the Cahuilla warrior said quietly. 'His horse is shod and he wears boots instead of moccasins. I would guess he's from Mexico. Sand Papago maybe, or Yaqui.'

'That'd be my guess, too. Let me know if you see any more sign, will you? I don't like people dogging my tracks.'

'I know the feeling.'

'Is it far to where Huarache hunts?'

Lagarto cocked his head at the question and shrugged. 'We'll be there this afternoon.'

They rode out on to the sage-covered flats east of the San Jacinto range, riding slowly to spare the horses in the heat of the day, and keeping a wary eye on their back trail.

It was early afternoon when they turned into a wide, rock-cluttered arroyo, worked past the sharp agave spears and clumps of teddy bear cholla near the entrance, and rode slowly up the slope on an age-old game trail.

The heat being reflected from the shattered grey rocks of the arroyo was almost unbearable, the horses chuffing at the intensity of it but plodding steadily on toward a shield of pale shadows a little farther in.

A fat rock squirrel perched on a boulder gave a series of high-pitched barks as they passed by, then flicked away out of sight behind the rock. High overhead a pair of red-tailed hawks soared in effortless circles on the rising currents of air and they could hear the raucous calls of a raven somewhere farther up the valley.

The game trail made a switchback to the east, another back toward the west, climbed steadily for about a mile, and finally topped out on a rounded ridge.

The air on the ridge was decidedly cooler than it had been in the valley and carried the smell of juniper and pinyon pine.

After another half-mile, the game trail came to an abrupt end at an oasis of fan palms clustered in a grove around a deep, shaded pool of water.

There were several Cahuilla warriors scattered around the shadowed oasis, tending the central cook fire, skinning game, or simply sleeping in the shade. Lagarto acknowledged them with nods and soft words as he slid down from his horse.

Ned, too, stepped down from his horse, glancing up at the loose crowns of the palms, the lower canopy of scrub oak, and the deep grass where the Indian ponies were picketed.

It would be, he decided, a good place to pitch camp for the night and he turned to help Dolores down from the sorrel.

'Is your friend here?' she asked, brushing a strand of hair away from her face.

'I don't see him, but I'm sure he's around somewhere.'

She rolled her eyes at his reply, turned on her heel, and paced away to an empty spot in the shade.

Lagarto didn't comment on her behavior, apparently out of pure politeness, but Ned saw the doubting question in his eyes.

He had questions, too.

'Are you hungry?' Lagarto asked softly. 'We have some venison roasting.'

'I could eat.'

'I'll have one of the young men bring some for you,' the warrior said. He turned and paced away toward the fire.

Ned felt the wave of shame and anger swamping his mind, and wasn't able to contain it.

Dolores was acting the bitch and it was time to end it.

Turning slowly, he let his gaze settle on her, seated on a weathered palm log beneath the trees, spinning her parasol above her head. He decided he'd had all he was going to take.

'What's the hell's wrong with you?' he demanded.

'What do you mean?'

'You're making me ashamed. These people expect their women to do a little more than just sit around putting on airs. They have invited us into their camp to share their food and give us protection and you park yourself in the shade and act as if, somehow, you've been insulted.'

'How *should* I act,' she asked defiantly.

He narrowed his eyes, studying her. 'Maybe you could show a little gratitude, maybe try to help out a little.'

'I'm not comfortable being here.'

He huffed quietly at her response. 'I don't really give a damn whether you're comfortable or not, missy. You're not in your big hacienda in Jalisco now. You're in the middle of the Yuha badlands and it's time you woke up to the reality of it.'

She lowered her eyes after a moment and hesitated before replying. 'I'm sorry.'

'No, you're not,' he said flatly. 'If you were you wouldn't be sitting there. You'd be gathering firewood or tending to the horses. Something. You damn sure aren't earning any respect from the Indians by doing what you're doing now.'

She lifted her eyes slowly, like a child being caught writing bad words on the chalkboard at school. 'I've never been in a situation like this.'

'A situation like what?'

'I don't know. Surrounded by savages, not understanding their ways.'

Ned nodded ponderously, peering at her through narrowed eyes. 'Well, you better figure it out in a real quick hurry, miss. Much more of this stupidity, I'll just ride out and you can try to find the treasure ship on your own.'

'You wouldn't dare,' she muttered.

'Oh, wouldn't I?'

A young-looking warrior approached them quietly, holding out a small clay bowl. '*Sukat*,' he mumbled, glancing down. '*Sukat*.'

'I think he's telling us it's venison,' Ned said softly. 'Either that or he's telling us to eat.'

'But there are no utensils,' Dolores groused over her shoulder.

Ned accepted the bowls, handed one to the woman sitting complacently on the log, and bobbed his head in thanks to the young warrior.

'I told you a minute ago to wake up, lady. God made fingers long before he made forks and spoons. And, if eating with your fingers is good enough for these people, it's good enough for the likes of us.'

She shook her head sadly and picked a piece of

roast venison out of the bowl. 'My family will never believe this.'

He snorted. 'That's their problem.'

CHAPTER EIGHT

There was a slight clamoring of voices from near the cook fire, and Ned glanced up in time to see Huarache, his old Cahuilla friend, step out of the waist-high manzanita brush and amble around the fire toward him.

He looked old now, his long hair streaked with grey and moving in the soft breeze off the mountains. He wore nothing but a pair of unbleached cotton pants, a dried-acorn necklace, and a broken-toothed grin.

He knew Huarache had been schooled at one of the missions over on the coast; he had always been impressed by how well the old man spoke English.

'Long time you don't come to the land of Huarache, Ned Gamble,' the old warrior said flatly. 'It is good to see you again.'

'It's good to see you again, too, my friend,' Ned answered pushing himself to his feet and extending a hand. 'How have you been?'

'I'm OK.'

'Please,' he told the Cahuilla elder, 'sit down for a while. We have much to talk about.'

The Cahuilla elder lowered himself to the fan-palm log close to Dolores, rested his elbows on his knees, and let his blunt fingers dangle toward the ground.

'What happened to your neck?' he asked quietly. 'Somebody try to cut your throat?'

Ned reached up and touched the arrow wound on the side of his neck, a little surprised that the old warrior had noticed it. 'No, we had a little set-to with some Mojave braves down at Yuha Well a couple of nights ago. They stole our horses and I caught up to them at Carrizo Creek.'

'You sure they Mojave?'

'Yeah, they all had the blue face tattoos.'

The old warrior nodded. 'Strange people, the Mojave. They don't like fighting but they have what they call *kwanamis*, brave men, among them. For them it is a way of life. They have strange dreams and think the dream spirits give them special powers.'

That was easy enough to believe.

He remembered all too well the insane look in the eyes of the warrior who had attacked him with nothing but a war club.

'They think some kind of judge looks at them when they come to the Land of the Dead. If a man goes there with no blue marks on his face, his spirit comes back to earth and will live in a rat hole for ever.'

'Now that is strange,' Ned mumbled.

'Have you eaten?'

'Yes, just a little while ago. One of your young men brought us some venison.'

'I have some acorn bread,' the Cahuilla elder added softly. 'You don't need no teeth to chew it.'

He turned slightly and scanned Dolores from head to foot rather blatantly. 'This your woman?'

'No,' Ned said. 'I'm just her guide.'

'Good thing. She's not strong enough for you.'

Ned saw the sudden venom hit Dolores' eyes and realized, with another shocking surge of insight into her character, that she would never, ever befriend the old man.

Her arrogance stunned him again within a matter of only a few minutes and he wasn't so sure he could forgive her for her behavior.

It just served to strengthen the misgivings he already had.

Ned leveled his gaze at the Cahuilla elder. 'Can we take a walk, my friend? There is something I'd like to discuss with you.'

'Of course,' Huarache said softly. 'Come, I will show you the waterfall.'

He rose and paced back toward the fire and the group of warriors sitting on their haunches in the dappled shade.

Ned knew Huarache was not considered the chief of the band, still, the respect shown to him as an elder of the tribe was amazing, and every one of the other men bobbed their heads or spoke a soft greeting to him as he passed.

He followed the ageing warrior around the edge of the deep pool and on past the fire, leaving Dolores seated in the shade of the fan palms and staring morosely after them.

'My friend,' he said when they were out of earshot, 'the first time we met you told me a story handed down from the Old Ones about the first time the Cahuilla people had ever seen the white man.'

'Yes,' Huarache said with a somber nod, 'I remember. The story of great white bird.'

'Do you think the story is true or is it just something to entertain the children?'

'Oh, it's true,' he insisted. 'Very true.'

Ned took a deep breath, relieved at the news, and exhaled heavily.

'Would you happen to know where the white bird is?'

A look of surprise washed over the old warrior's face, as if he couldn't quite believe the question.

'Well, of course I do. I've been there many times.'

Again Ned felt a surge of relief. This treasure hunt might possibly pan out after all.

'I wonder if you'd mind telling me where it is? I have an idea it might be exactly what this young woman is looking for.'

Huarache shrugged his narrow shoulders and spoke softly, almost reverently. 'There's not much left of it now, Ned. Just the skeleton and it's covered with sand.'

'Still,' Ned said, 'I'd like to see it.'

The old Cahuilla lifted his hands in resignation. 'It's not hard to find. There's a trail made by the Ancient Ones just east of the ridgeline that goes from one spring to the next. Three springs down from here you will find another pool with many palms. Good water there and grazing for the horses. We call the place *Pa'at Kawís,* Sheep Mountain, and the white bird is in the canyon just below the spring.'

'And how do I find the ancient trail?'

Huarache ducked his chin at a slight opening in the brush just beyond the fan palms surrounding the pool. 'It starts right there. Just follow that up the ridge, maybe two miles, and it will lead you into another trail – always looks white in the afternoon sun – that runs south along the ridge. Good hunting down there, too.'

'That's good to know,' Ned mumbled. 'We could use some camp meat.'

'Want me to show you?'

'No.' Ned shook his head. 'I think I can find it.'

'Take some of that acorn bread with you, Ned,' the Cahuilla elder prodded. 'My wife made it.'

Ned glanced away at the ridgeline above them. 'You say that other trail always looks white in the afternoon sun?'

'You'll recognize it when you see it. Easy walking.'

'Then I guess I'd better get started while we still have some light.'

The ageing warrior nodded his understanding and clapped Ned on the shoulder with a grizzled hand.

91

'And don't ride away from the land of Huarache without saying goodbye this time, Ned. There's no telling when we'll see each other again.'

'Or,' Ned said somberly, 'if we even will.'

CHAPTER NINE

It was just as Huarache had told him: the ancient trail looked white in the afternoon sun and was crowded on both sides by a thick covering of red-barked manzanita and milkweed. In places the trail ran through the dappled shade of juniper and ponderosa pine groves and the air was heavy with their scent.

A small flock of birds flicked through the low-hanging branches and a mule deer stood, head up and alert, a few yards back into the trees watching them pass.

Ned rode slowly, stopping often to look and listen, but nothing around them seemed out of the ordinary.

Dolores Torreón trailed along a few yards behind him, sullen and quiet; he could almost feel the distaste she harbored for these surroundings.

Old Huarache had been right, she wasn't strong enough, and there was precious little Ned Gamble could do about it.

He spotted the telltale fronds of fan-palms from a quarter of a mile up the trail and heaved a deep sigh of relief. It had been a long day and he was more than ready for some hot food and a good night's sleep.

Even the grulla seemed to sense the day's journey was over. She whickered quietly at the smell of water and quickened her pace.

Ned reined in at the edge of a deep, clear pool of mountain spring water and glanced around at the grove of palms. A lower canopy of oak and man-zanita cut off the view of the ridgeline above them but the slope dropped off sharply to the east.

'Must be the place,' he said quietly. 'Three springs down, like old Huarache said.'

'I didn't like him,' Dolores muttered half under her breath. 'Who does he think he is to pass judge-ment on me?'

He turned and studied her through narrowed eyes. Had he heard her right?

'He was probably comparing you to an Indian woman.'

'Still,' she said, pouting, 'it wasn't his place to judge me.'

Ned shrugged and let the conversation go. He stepped down from the saddle, and had to help her down from the sorrel yet again.

Without a word he stripped the gear off the horses, led them to water, then staked them out in a patch of grass near the pool.

Dolores had eased herself down on to a palm log

in the shade, just as she had at the Cahuilla camp, watching him with her hands folded demurely in her lap.

'Might as well see what we can see while we've still got some daylight,' he rumbled.

He turned away from her and paced across to the steep drop off above a narrow, rock-ribbed gorge. He became wide-eyed at what he saw in the little canyon.

Below him was the unmistakable outline of a ship with yellow-grey sandstone formed around its bow. One cracked grey pole jutted up into the desert air with a single yardarm still attached and hanging at a steep angle.

'Well, I'll be damned,' he muttered, turning back toward her. 'I haven't been around the ocean much in my life, but that is definitely a ship down there.'

She scurried to his side at the statement, wide-eyed, and peered down into the gorge, just as he was doing.

'You knew about this all along, didn't you?' she asked close to his shoulder.

Her words had the ring of suspicion about them and, for some murky reason, his instincts told him to be wary.

'I had an idea.'

'Well, at least the book was right,' she purred. 'This canyon would have been a nearly landlocked cove and sheltered from the wind and seas.'

He glanced at her over his shoulder, wondering why she had ever held that information back when she'd read to him from the book.

Realistically, there was nothing he could say.

He'd held back information from her, too.

'It's pretty much buried in sand,' he said evenly. 'You can just make out the corner of a cargo hatch on the main deck there and that's where I'll start digging.'

'It's going to be a lot of work.'

'You got that part right, lady, but that will be tomorrow. Right now we need to get a fire going and start some food.'

'I take it that means firewood,' she groused.

'And lots of it, I've got a feeling we'll be here a while.'

The half-breed slid down from his horse, headed straight for the kettle of beans on the rock beside the fire, and scooped himself up a hefty plateful.

'I'm so hungry right now I could eat the ass off a skunk!'

'You trail them?' Barajas asked from his seat.

'All damned day,' Indio muttered, shoveling a spoonful of beans into his mouth. 'It's hotter'n blue blazes out there and nothing but a horse's belly for shade.'

'So?' Manny prodded, 'What did you find?'

'Some local Indian took them north to another canyon and they trailed up that to a pool of water under a stand of palm trees.'

He took another bite and spoke around a mouthful of beans. 'Sign on the ground said there'd been a big Indian hunting party camped there, but they left and we can probably move our own camp over there tonight.'

Barajas squinted at him, wondering why he didn't give him the information he really wanted. 'What about Dolores and the gringo?'

'They moved on. Rode up to another trail just below the ridgeline and turned south. They're easy enough to track, you know? One of their horses always drags his left hind hoof.'

'How far is it?'

'To the pool?' Indio shrugged at the question. 'Three, four hours. We can make it before dark and it'll be a better place to camp than this.'

'We'd better get moving, then. Sun's already starting to go down.'

He turned to the rest of the men and nodded. 'Saddle up, *muchachos*. It's time to ride. Diego, dump out the frijoles, clean up the utensils, and pack them. Miguel, take Indio's horse to water, he's been out in this damned heat all day. Pepe, douse the fire.'

Spinning on his heel, Manny leveled his eyes at the half-breed.

'I know you, Indio,' he said quietly. 'You got some kind of a feeling about this that you're not talking about. What is it?'

Indio shrugged his narrow shoulders again and fed another spoonful of beans into his mouth. 'I think the gringo is on to something, Manny.'

'What makes you say that?'

'Well, think about it. He's been pushing north for two days. Ever since Yuha Well. And now he's turned back south?'

Barajas pursed his thin lips and narrowed his eyes. 'Yeah, I see what you mean. That *does* have a funny ring to it.'

'Damn right it does. Tracking ain't all that hard, Manny. You just have to remember that nothing moves in the desert without a reason.'

'Yeah?'

'Yeah. But the reason can be anything, you know? Love, hate, war, water, gold, anything at all. And if you can figure out *why* something moved, it ain't all that hard to figure out *where*.'

Manny threw his hands up in resignation. 'I still don't get it.'

'Think about it, boss man. If they're sitting there in the shade of the palm trees, a nice cool breeze coming down off the mountains, plenty of food and water to hand and good grazing for their horses, why the hell would they pull out?'

'The pearls?'

'It's the only thing that makes sense.'

'Damn!' Barajas breathed. 'He could have the pearls and be gone before we even get there.'

He jogged away toward his big buckskin, threw the blanket and saddle on, and climbed quickly into the saddle.

'*Date prisa, muchachos!*' he shouted. 'Hurry up, boys! It's time to ride.'

Indio handed his empty plate to Diego, who was

still wiping the residue of dried beans off the other plates, and sauntered casually away toward his pinto.

'Man's going to put himself into an early grave,' he said to no one.

They rode up the rock-cluttered valley in the long shadows of the peaks to the west. The chill night wind was already drifting down the slope and Manny hunched a little deeper into the collar of his duster for the warmth.

He didn't like the looks of the palm oasis when they eventually reined in. There was so much Indian sign around – unshod hoof marks and moccasin prints – that even he could read it.

And he was definitely no hand at reading sign.

He sat his horse at the edge of the deep pool for several minutes, eyeing the place suspiciously. After some moments he swung down from the saddle and fixed the half-breed with hooded eyes.

'You're sure there's none of them still around?' he asked the tracker.

'Relax, Manny,' Indio replied. 'You can bet they know we're here, probably watching us at this very minute, but, as long as we don't make any threatening moves in their direction, they'll leave us alone.'

'I don't trust them.'

Indio snorted. 'That makes it about even then. Chances are they don't trust you, either. We're in their home country now and that means they have the edge. Just play it close to the chest, don't do anything stupid, and we'll be all right.'

Manny's voice cracked like a dry willow when he spoke. 'You'd better hope you're right.'

Indio narrowed his eyes at the slender *vaquero*. 'I grew up with a bunch of wild-assed Indians, Manny. The kind that would just as soon kill you as look at you. You might want to keep that in mind before you start threatening me.'

Barajas stiffened slightly. The 'breed had never spoken to him in such a manner and it unnerved him.

'I didn't mean anything by it,' he mumbled.

'Yeah? Well, it sounded to me like you did.'

Indio turned on his heel and paced away toward the sound of a waterfall, his long black hair waving across his shoulders. There was no doubt in Manny's mind that the wiry half-breed wouldn't hesitate a minute to kill him.

It was an eye opening revelation.

Clouds were piling up over the peaks and ridges west of them and the air was growing steadily colder in the gathering darkness.

'Get a fire going,' he ordered, 'and take care of the horses. Diego, you're cooking again. Paco, find a place on the trail coming in here and stand guard for a while. I need some time to think.'

He turned away from the others, looking for a good place to rest, and paced silently away toward a grey palm log.

This whole venture was starting to wear on him and he knew he was near his breaking-point.

It had all seemed so simple back in Guerrero: put

Dolores on a stagecoach for the north and he and his men would follow on horseback. They were *caballeros*, after all. What could be more natural than that?

Yet, somehow, it had never occurred to him how far it was from Acapulco to Heroica Nogales, how many nights he would have to sleep on the ground and eat tasteless food.

He prayed that Indio had been right, that this gringo desert rat really was on to something.

If it was true it meant this hellish journey was coming to an end, that there might be only a few more days of it to endure, and he could be headed home.

It felt like a breath of air to a drowning man.

Then he realized, amazingly, that *he* was the drowning man.

It would not do to alienate Indio, he decided. The man could turn on him in a heartbeat.

He had absolutely nothing to lose.

Dawn came early to the ridges of the San Jacinto range, sunlight hitting the higher peaks first then quickly sliding down the slope as the morning sun lifted above the Chocolate Mountains several miles to the east.

There didn't seem to be as much sound from the night-time hunters in the mountains as there was on the desert floor. The thrashing of dried palm fronds in the gusty downslope wind had disturbed him some time after midnight, but he had gotten a good night's sleep and felt rested when he finally rolled out.

He piled a handful of tinder between the smoke-blackened rocks, touched it with a lucifer from his shirt pocket, and had a small smokeless fire going again in a matter of minutes.

He slid the coffee pot and the kettle of leftover beans to the edge of the rock where they'd heat up slowly, then he sat back on his heels to study their surroundings.

The skirts of dead leaves hanging down against the trunks of the fan palms blocked his view of the ridge to the west, but to the north and south, as far as the eye could see, the land was covered with stands of juniper and pine and gigantic clusters of rock.

He glanced east into the wide swath of sun-glint on Lake Cahuilla and counted his blessings that he would be slightly above some of the heat that would be building down there today.

Dolores stretched and rolled on her blankets, her clothes rumpled and dirty now, her hair in tangled strings; he knew without asking that she was in a sour mood when she eventually sat up.

'You hungry?' he asked across the fire.

She stared at him for a long minute, almost as if she were searching for the words. 'I am,' she mumbled then, 'but I don't think I can eat any more of your bacon and beans.'

He nodded his understanding. Truth be known, he felt the same way himself.

'Well, we've still got some of that acorn bread Huarache gave us.'

'Yes,' she said glancing away. 'Maybe I'll have some of that.'

He turned and fixed her with narrowed eyes. 'Well, help yourself to it, missy. I didn't suddenly become your servant.'

He picked up one of the chipped enamel plates, scooped himself up a ladleful of beans, splashed some of the warmed-up coffee into his cup, and paced away to sit by himself on the palm log at the edge of the manzanita thicket.

It was going to be a long day.

CHAPTER TEN

Ned picked old Frank's scoop shovel out of the pack and rump-slid down the steep incline, braking himself as best he could and watching the small avalanche of sand and gravel tumble down ahead of him. Eventually he came to a stop with his feet braced against the exposed gunwale of the ancient caravel.

Gingerly he reached over the rail and stabbed the shovel at what he could see of the deck, testing whether it was safe to walk on. It seemed solid enough to his way of thinking and he eased himself over the gunwale to stand on the cracked, grey planking.

Two and a half centuries since anyone had stood on this deck, he mused, glancing around at the steep rock walls of the gorge. Two and a half centuries of wind and heat and dust.

The sailors who'd served aboard her must have felt totally dispossessed when they had to scramble over the side and abandon ship. Everything they knew, everything familiar, their security, their possessions, would have been left behind, while they faced the prospect of straggling across a hundred miles of the most inhospitable landscape known to man, in order just to survive.

He paced gingerly across to the exposed corner of the cargo hatch, then prodded at the heap of sand and wind-blown gravel that had piled up there over the years.

It was crusty, starting to solidify into sandstone, but still loose enough for him to get the blade of the shovel into it. He stabbed at the pile, breaking off fist-sized chunks, and sending small cascades of sand and gravel trickling down to the ancient deck.

He worked steadily, throwing the detritus as far to the side as he could and stopping only to take an occasional swig of water from the blanket-covered canteen.

He was fully aware that Dolores stood complacently at the edge of the drop-off high above him, twirling her fancy French parasol above her head, and watching him work.

He could understand her apprehension.

The future of her entire family hung in the balance here, depending on whether they found the pearls, whether there *were* any pearls to be found, and whether or not they could get them out.

To be sure it was a noble cause she had undertaken.

Just a crying, damned shame she wasn't behaving nobly.

By mid-morning he had cleared a section of the conglomerate about a yard wide from one end of the hatch to the other – big enough for a man of his size to drop down into – and could feel his shirt sticking uncomfortably to the perspiration that was sheeting down his back.

The hatch appeared to have been covered with some kind of tarpaulin at one time, but that had disintegrated over the years and all that remained of it now was a tattered ribbon of fabric along the edge.

Using the blade of old Frank's shovel, he hammered up the wooden wedges holding the batten in place and tossed them on to the deep pile of sand he'd created. Then he paused for a moment and wiped the sweatband of his hat.

He stripped away the brittle batten and prised the long grey planks of the hatch cover off one at a time.

As he leaned in over the hatch coaming he could make out the pillows of sand that had filtered down through the cracks over the centuries, but the cargo hold itself was dark in shadow and he could see little else.

With the scorching sun glaring down on him from a brassy, cloudless sky, he scrambled back up the steep slope to the palm oasis for a breather and a cup of hot black coffee.

'That looks like a lot of work down there,' Dolores mumbled from the shade.

He squinted at her words, a question flooding his mind. . . .

106

If it looked like a lot of work, why the hell wasn't she helping?

'You got that part right,' he retorted. 'Still, if it's worth having, it's worth working for.'

'Are you convinced now that this is worth the effort?'

'It is to me. I've been living on bacon and beans for so many years it makes my nose bleed just to think about it. With a poke full of money I might be able to afford a juicy steak with all the trimmings once in a while.'

She had nothing further to say, just turned away and gazed into the dust-hazy distance of the Yuha desert.

Her attitude was starting to bother him.

He dipped a potful of water from the clear pool, dropped in a handful of grounds, and set it next to the fire to heat up, a little dismayed that this Dolores Torreón had absolutely nothing to offer a man in the way of help.

Was gathering firewood all she could do?

There wouldn't be much call for that on some caballero's estate in old Jalisco, now would there?

'I got the hatch opened up,' he said after a few moments. 'Have you got something to put the pearls in if I find any down there?'

Her eyes went wide with sudden interest then, and she shifted her look back to him. 'Did you see anything?'

'Not yet. It's too dark in the hold, but I don't intend to scramble back up that slope every five minutes if I do find something.'

She nodded, showing some enthusiasm at last. 'Give me a minute.'

'No hurry,' he said. 'I'm going to have another cup of coffee before I go back down.'

She sauntered around the fire to the big leather aparejo the dapple grey had been carrying, dug around its contents for a moment, then paced back with a stack of folded denim bags in her arms.

'There should be ten of them there,' she purred, 'all with drawstrings. I had no idea how many pearls we'd find. My great-great-grandfather said only that it was beyond imagination.'

Ned poured himself another shot of coffee, took a sip, and rose to his full height. 'Well, we're about to find out.'

He took the armload of sacks from her, rump-slid down the slope again, stepped over the gunwale, and stood once more on the age-old caravel's main deck.

He dropped the shovel into the dim interior of the hold then eased himself over the hatch coaming and let go.

He landed softly on a hummock of sifted sand and sat for a long minute, letting his eyes become accustomed to the shadows.

There were six big baskets that he could see from where he sat, brittle and dry with age, jutting up from the heaps of sand and dust that had sifted down through the cracked deck over the years.

He crawled slowly across the hold and began fanning at them with his sweat-stained hat, whisking away the thin layer of dust that covered them and trying not to breathe the haze of dust motes that filled the air.

Once the baskets were exposed, he simply sat back on his haunches, rested his chin on the side of his fist, and peered at them with narrowed eyes.

Three of the baskets held only lustrous black pearls, two held nothing but white, and one was heaped to the rim with blue and greenish pearls, which he had never even heard of before.

He exhaled heavily at the sight, his mind reeling at the prospect of what life could be after he sold off his share of the treasure trove sitting before him.

It was hard to imagine.

He glanced up at the narrow shafts of sunlight filtering down through the cracks in the ancient deck, the shadows that flooded the compartment, and forced himself back to the reality of the moment.

The pearls represented more money than he'd ever even considered.

The problem now was how to get them out.

He knew he wouldn't be able to jump as high as the hatch coaming and haul himself out, especially not with a sack full of pearls in one hand, but there had to be a way.

There were a few incredibly old sea chests showing above the heaps of sand in the shadowy hold, but he thought it likely they'd be full of clothing and the personal belongings of the seamen who'd served about the caravel and would be too heavy to move.

After a moment he spotted the end of a large wooden keg showing above the mound of sand piled up against the forward bulkhead. The protruding spigot said it had been a water barrel at one time, or possibly a keg of wine.

If. . . ?

He crawled across to it on his hands and knees, rapped on the top, and breathed a great sigh of relief at the hollow sound it gave off.

It was empty.

He scrambled back across the hold for the shovel and set to work digging the keg out of the sand.

Even more whitish dust motes filled the stagnant air of the hold as he dug, clogging his nostrils, coating his clothes, and sticking to his sweaty skin. The only sound was the chunk of his shovel driving into the detritus and the hushed whisper of sliding sand every time he threw a shovelful of it to the side.

When he thought he'd cleared away enough of the sand heap to make a difference, he gripped the top of the keg with hard hands, tipping and pulling until it came free and he was able to roll it across to the opening in the hatch.

He sat back, breathing heavily, wiped the sweatband of his hat yet again, and pondered his next move.

There was little doubt in his mind that Dolores would still be watching from the top of the slope and he found it a little odd that she'd come out here prepared to haul away whatever treasure they found, but not for anything else.

He shrugged the thought off, picked up a couple of the sacks, and scrambled back across to the baskets.

Careful that he didn't spill any of the precious pearls that he'd found on to the sand, he started scooping double handfuls of them out of the brittle baskets and dribbling them down into the wide-open mouth of a sack.

After filling the first bag almost to the point of overflowing he pulled the drawstring tight, tied it in a quick knot, and spread the next sack.

It was a slower process than he would have liked but it had to be done.

God knew, he'd never have another chance like this and he had to make this one count.

Eight bags emptied the baskets and, standing on the end of the upturned water keg, he boosted them one at a time up over the hatch coaming to the greyed deck of the ancient craft.

At last he hauled himself out and sat on one of the bags for a long minute. He wiped the thin film of dust away from his mouth and nose and glanced up the slope toward their encampment.

She was up there, all right, standing hipshot in the shadow of a palm, and he could clearly see the anxiety on her face.

He couldn't blame her for what she was feeling.

It had obviously been a long ordeal for her to endure and it was, at long, long last winding down.

It would be winding down for him, too, he mused. Once he'd sold his portion of the treasure, he'd have more than enough to start the horse ranch on the coast, more than enough to live in comfort for the rest of his life, and, no matter what else came to pass, he would never have to eat bacon and beans again.

He grimaced at the thought, picked up the canteen from where he'd set it in the sand, and took another long swig.

Yes, sir, by God. It had been a long time in coming.

He hoisted a heavy sack of pearls in each hand and started up the slope, slipping, falling to his knees, forcing himself back up, slogging a few more steps toward the top, and finally stumbling over the edge, whipped and gasping for breath.

He dragged the sacks a few feet further and sagged to his knees.

'God damn,' he groaned. 'That'll take the starch out of you.'

'Is that all of them?' Dolores asked from the shade.

He snorted. 'Not by a long sight. I've got probably three more trips to make up that slope and it's not going to get any easier.'

'Is there anything I can do to help?'

Ned exhaled heavily and wagged his head in dismay at her question. Was the woman really that harebrained?

'Not unless you want to haul a couple of sacks up that hill.'

She shrugged and raised her hands in surrender.

'I don't think I could.'

He nodded his agreement and leaned back against a boulder. 'If you really want to help, try keeping the coffee hot. A few more trips like that last one and I'm going to call it a day.'

'A few more trips like that last one is all we need,' she murmured.

Again he nodded. 'You're right on that one. A few more trips up that slope and we'll ride out of here rich as kings and there's no reason to drag my feet on getting it done.'

He pushed himself up to his full height, flexed his shoulder muscles, and trudged back over the edge of the hill.

With only a moment's hesitation on the ancient ship's deck, he hoisted two more bags of pearls and slogged his way back up the torturous slope. This time, however, he didn't stop to rest.

Instead, he wiped his face with his ragged blue bandanna, took a moment to catch his breath, and started down the slope for the third time.

The work was starting to tell on him. His breathing had become ragged and shallow, his arms aching and leaden, his legs trembling slightly at the strain, and he knew he couldn't stop.

There was still a sight of work to be done, more struggle staring him in the face, and there was no one he could turn to.

The Torreón woman simply stood in the shade of the palms, watching him labor, offering not the slightest bit of sympathy or concern, and it chafed

113

against everything he believed in.

He dropped to his knees at the top of the slope, breathing heavily, trying to clear his vision, and praying to everything that was holy that he had another climb hill still in him.

Dolores had nothing to say and that suited him just fine.

He plodded over the edge again, his final trip, rump-slid down through the cascading gravel, and stood straddle-legged one last time on the brittle deck.

The ancient caravel seemed almost familiar to him now, as though he had actually served on her when she was still under sail, and he thought he felt the same melancholy that those long-ago sailors must have felt when they were ordered to abandon ship.

He glanced around to the east, where the rolling seas would have come from all those years ago, shrugged his shoulders, and hoisted the last two sacks.

One more climb, he thought. Just one more climb.

CHAPTER ELEVEN

There were six of them.

Hard, belted men from south of the border, the kind the Federales would be interested in, and they sat their mounts in a rough line, gazing at him in total disdain, as if he were a pack animal or a simple *peón* tending a patch of beans.

Dolores sprang to her feet smiling insanely the moment they reined in, scurried around the campfire, and laid her hand on the center rider's thigh.

'Oh, my God, Manny,' she moaned, 'am I glad to see you!'

Ned's forehead furrowed into a frown.

What the hell was that all about?

She *knew* this guy?

Another of them, a pot-bellied man wearing an embroidered grey sombrero, turned slightly to the side and mumbled a quick question. '*Quieres que lo mate*, Manny?'

The *vaquero* on his left, the one Dolores had run to, raised a hand and answered without looking away. 'Not yet.'

Ned's Spanish wasn't perfect, he was well aware of that, but he was pretty sure the paunchy one had asked this Manny if he should kill him.

The other one – Manny – had replied in such an offhand way that Ned knew his death was a small part of a much bigger picture. It had already been planned out.

And he didn't like the feeling.

Manny.

That would be the Manny Barajas whom old Frank Dougherty at the livery stable had mentioned. The leader of this ragtag bunch.

His face was gaunt and mustachioed, his eyes a little too close together, and he wore a constant sneer, as if he always smelled something bad.

'Please, get me out of here, Manny,' Dolores whined loudly. 'This whole thing has been a nightmare.'

'In good time, little one,' the slope-shouldered *vaquero* replied. He nodded toward the denim sacks lined up beyond the fire. 'Are those the pearls?'

'Yes,' she answered, 'eight sacks of them.'

Manny bobbed his head and spoke over his shoulder. 'Get them, Paco.'

One of the men swung down from his saddle and started toward the sacks. Ned stopped him with an uplifted hand.

'What the hell's going on here?' he asked evenly. 'And how the hell did you get my horses?'

'These horses, *señor*?' the pot-bellied *vaquero*

116

chimed in. 'The old man at the stable didn't know who they belonged to. At least he didn't say.'

Ned cocked his head, reading a deeper meaning into pot-belly's words. 'You killed old Frank?'

'His time had come, *señor*.'

'Like you, gringo,' Barajas interrupted. 'You're very close to death but apparently you don't realize it.'

'I take a lot of killing, mister.'

Without another word, Ned drew and fired, watching with grim satisfaction as the paunchy *vaquero* with the embroidered sombrero and the smart mouth toppled backward over his horse's rump, dead before he hit the ground.

Ned spun on his heel, legs driving, dove over the edge of the slope, and landed on his shoulder. He rolled to his feet in a desperate, stumbling run toward the ancient caravel.

It was his only hope.

He felt the burning stab of pain as a bullet ripped through his side. He staggered a few more steps to the caravel's deck, and pitched headlong over the hatch coaming on to the deep mounds of sifted sand in the hold.

He landed flat on his back with a powerful grunt, lay there close to blacking out for a moment, then twisted sideways into the darker shadows close to the hull.

Without a second's hesitation he flipped open the loading gate of the big Colt Peacemaker, ejected the spent casing, and rammed another round into the cylinder.

Clamping his teeth hard together, he braced the pistol against his knee and squinted up through the opening he'd made in the hatch cover.

No matter what else came to pass, by God, he wasn't going down without a fight.

He felt the blood oozing out of the bullet hole in his side, soaking the shirt, plastering it to his ribs, and there was precious little he could do about it.

He dragged the ragged blue bandanna from out of his pocket and pressed it down hard over the wound, hoping to stem the flow of blood, but his eyes remained fixed on the hatch.

Several minutes slipped by in the deathly quiet of the hold before he heard the unmistakable jingle of big-roweled Mexican spurs and the hushed thud of footfalls on the deck above him.

So it had come down to this, had it?

A man he didn't know hunting him down? Backing him into a corner and shooting him like a rabid dog?

Well, it wouldn't be quite that easy, *compadre*.

It was like he'd told Manny Barajas a few minutes ago: he took a lot of killing.

A trickle of sand sifted down through the cracks in the ancient deck each time the man up there moved. It marked his location as accurately as a pointed finger, and, as near as Ned could tell, there was only one man on board.

'Leave him, Pepe,' Barajas called down the slope. 'He is already dead and too dumb to know it.'

'A minute only, Manny,' Pepe shouted back. 'He's

a sitting duck down there.'

Ned hesitated only long enough to see the *vaquero*'s shadow move above him again. He lifted the Peacemaker and squeezed off a shot through the brittle planking of the deck.

He narrowed his eyes grimly at the sound of the man's body slumping to the deck and nodded soberly as spatters of blood dripping through the cracks started making small pock marks in the heap of sand below decks.

'Fool!' Barajas yelled. 'I told you to leave him.'

That angry outburst was followed by another terse command.

'*Vamos*! We go!'

Then the pounding of horse's hoofs came to him in the stifling heat of the hold, trailing away up Sheep Mountain.

Suddenly there was no sound.

Only the overwhelming quiet of the high country.

Still he waited several minutes, huddled tensely against the brittle hull of the old caravel, before he moved.

He dabbed at the blood still leaking from his side, pressed the bandanna hard against the bullet hole for several minutes, and wagged his head in dismay.

There wasn't much more he could do, and it was time to move.

He pushed himself slowly up to his knees, wincing at the burning pain below his ribcage, and edged crabwise toward the narrow shaft of sunlight stabbing down into the darkness of the hold.

It would be just like Barajas to leave a gunman hidden in the rocks up there to finish the job, he reflected, and he never had been much on trusting strangers.

The woman had gulled him, there was no doubt in his mind about that, and he wasn't the man to be easily fooled.

He had believed her story about the ranch in Jalisco – every damned word of it – and he'd believed she was above board and honorable about this whole venture.

The thing he couldn't quite get a grip on was the fact that she and Manny Barajas had been in it together all along, that the whole thing had been planned out in advance; he was the fall guy, and he hadn't seen it coming.

He stood cautiously below the opening he'd made in the hatch cover, set his low-crowned hat on the end of old Frank's scoop shovel, and pushed it into view above the coaming.

No shot rang out from the hillside above him and slowly – very slowly – he raised his head above the brittle wood.

It was quiet up there, almost too quiet, and he waited a long moment before gripping the lip of the hatch and pulling himself out on to the deck.

The *vaquero* he'd shot, the one Barajas had called Pepe, lay face down in the pile of sand Ned had raked off the hatch, his old Colt Army still in his fist, but he was long gone.

That was two of Manny's gang down for the count

and Ned felt not the slightest regret at killing either one of them.

They would have killed him without batting an eye and he knew it.

He took a minute picking the dead *vaquero*'s pistol out of his hand and thrusting it into the waistband of his trousers, another minute to strip the man of his gunbelt, grateful that it was full of .45 caliber ammunition, then scrambled over the side of the ship on to the loose soil of the slope.

The lousy bitch!

He'd done nothing to deserve this other than having the reputation for knowing his way around the desert. For damned sure he didn't have any of this coming.

He'd led the woman out here, found the ancient ship, and recovered the pearls for her. Everything she'd wanted from him.

It just made no sense.

Greed, he fumed. Avarice and greed.

It was the only thing that fitted.

Clawing his fingers into the rocky soil of the steep slope and scrabbling along on his knees, he dragged himself on up to the oasis, shoved his face into the clear water of the pool, and drank deeply.

It was a minor miracle he was still alive.

He sat in the shade of the fan palms for a long moment, surveying their little encampment beside the spring, the other dead *vaquero* lying there in the gravel, and trying to figure it out.

All the horses were gone, as were the pearls and

the supplies he'd brought along for the trail.

He was wounded and on foot on the edge of the barren Yuha desert and it was going to take some canny moves to make it out alive.

All he had to work with were the heavy Colt Peacemaker hanging on his hip, the pistol he'd stripped off Pepe, another on the body beside the slope, and a razor-sharp skinning knife hidden in a scabbard inside his boot.

He counted it a blessing that Barajas's men hadn't put out the fire.

Slowly, carefully, he lowered himself to the sand, fed another piece of manzanita into the coals and stared at it, almost in a daze, until it finally took hold and burst into flame.

He clenched his teeth hard together then and pondered the last several days.

What an absolute fool he'd been.

Old Frank had warned him about Manny Barajas and his men, had told him in plain English to watch his topknot out here, and he hadn't done it.

Now he was up against the odds.

It had come down to the point where push stands toe to toe with shove. And it was time for him to push back.

He had a score to settle with Manny Barajas and the woman, a big score, and it wasn't going to be pretty.

Forcing himself back to reality, he tugged his shirt out of his trousers and peered down to examine the wound.

The bleeding had already coagulated in the gash torn across his midsection and a surge of relief washed over him that he wouldn't have to cauterize it. He'd seen that grim procedure done in the wilderness a time or two and knew it involved some serious pain.

The smoke-blackened coffee pot still had a dab of coffee left in it, and Manny's men hadn't taken what was left of the bacon and beans.

At least he'd have a bite to eat and some hot, black coffee before the unwelcome challenge of survival began for him.

He set the coffee pot and Dutch oven slightly closer to the fire and fed some larger pieces of wood into the flame.

Then he heard the dull thud of a horse's hoofbeats plodding into his camp. He unshucked the long-barreled Peacemaker yet again. If it was one of Manny Barajas's men coming back to finish the job. . . .

He felt his eyes go wide as his friend, Huarache, the Cahuilla elder, walked his big sorrel mare through the manzanita brush beyond the pool.

'Huarache?' he mumbled. 'What are you doing here?'

'Watching,' the old warrior replied. 'Been watching you most of the day. From the hills.'

'Why didn't you come in to the fire?'

'I had fire.'

Ned pushed himself up, wincing at the sharp pain stabbing his side. 'Jesus, you're a sight for sore eyes.'

Huarache slid to the ground, ambled slowly round to the struggling fire, and eased himself down to sit on the greyed fan-palm log close beside him.

'Better let me take a look at that,' he said, ducking his head toward Ned's wound.

Ned nodded and lifted the bandanna away from the gash.

'It's stopped bleeding,' the elder murmured, 'but I think we'd better get you to Agua Caliente where we can put some medicine on it.'

He dragged a red stone pipe from his shirt pocket, tamped a small handful of tobacco into the bowl, and lit it with a brand from the fire.

'The little beads you brought from the great white bird,' he asked leveling his eyes at Ned, 'they are valuable?'

'Yes,' Ned replied. 'To the white man, they are very valuable.'

'Enough to kill for?'

'Apparently so,' Ned answered. 'Those bastards tried to kill me.'

The old warrior wagged his head but didn't avert his eyes. 'Strange breed, you white-eyes. Always killing warriors of your own tribe. It makes no sense.'

Ned could only nod his head at the old Cahuilla's words. There was no denying he was right.

'It's a big tribe, my friend, and some men deserve to die.'

'Still it is strange. When was the last time you ate?'

Ned shook his head dizzily and glanced away at the barren horizon east of them. 'Early this morning. Bacon and beans.'

'As I thought. I brought some roasted venison for you. You should eat to keep your strength up.'

'Damn,' Ned mumbled. 'I don't know what to say.'

The Cahuilla elder snorted at his words. 'We are taught never to visit a friend empty handed.'

Without another word Huarache ambled back to his sorrel, dug a piece of roasted back strap from his saddle-bag, and returned to the fire.

He eased himself down to the palm log again, sliced off a hunk of meat with a sharp skinning knife and held it out to Ned across the fire.

'The men who tried to kill you rode north, the way they came in,' he said easily. 'You will follow them?'

'I have to, my friend. They wronged me.'

'You will kill them?'

Ned didn't respond to the old one's question. The answer was obvious.

'I'll need a horse.'

'Take one of mine,' the ageing warrior droned. 'We'll ride double to Agua Caliente. My woman will look at your wound and feed you. You can leave when you're ready.'

Huarache pushed himself erect and paced away toward the pool. His sorrel mare lifted her head at his approach, whickered softly, and the Cahuilla elder heaved himself up on to her back.

'When you are ready,' he said quietly.

CHAPTER TWELVE

They rode several miles along the blanched trail of the Old Ones in silence, Ned holding a wad of Spanish moss he'd picked from the low-hanging branches of the oak trees to his side as a poultice. Huarache eyed the hills around them and guided the mare with his knees.

Shadows were reaching out already from the hills when they rode in to the oasis the Cahuilla hunting party had used the day before. Huarache walked the mare to the edge of the pool.

Ned dropped off the horse's rump, standing straddle-legged in the sand as the Cahuilla elder swung down and led the sorrel on to the water.

'The men who robbed you must have camped here last night,' he said quietly. He waved a wrinkled hand toward the shadows of the palms. 'Those ashes are new, and an Indian would never have built a fire that big below the palms. Palm fronds and sparks from a fire don't mix very well.'

Ned nodded soberly. 'I see your point.'

'It's not much farther to Agua Caliente now,' his ageing friend murmured, letting the mare tank up on water. 'Another couple of hours.'

'Sounds good to me. I wore myself down to a nubbin today.'

Huarache nodded. 'And all for nothing.'

He gave the sorrel another minute at the water, then tugged her head up and both men scrambled to her back. Huarache nudged her into a walk down the rock-strewn valley to the desert floor and spoke softly over his shoulder.

'The woman you were guiding didn't seem to resist very much when those men took her away. Did she know them?'

'Yes,' Ned mumbled. 'She called one of them by name. I'm guessing they had the whole thing planned out in advance.'

'It would not surprise me. It is said among my people that the white-eyes always plan their treachery.'

Ned couldn't argue with that. The story of the army's betrayal of Cochise at Apache Pass came to mind and there was just nothing he could say.

They fell into silence again and rode on just outside the fringe of the foothills.

He'd been to Huarache's house once before, on his first trip to the coast, and remembered well the forked upright posts supporting the roof beams, the palm-frond thatching, and the thin covering of sand that covered it.

It stood a little back from the spring, in the deep

shade of the fan-palm grove, smoke curled up from the metal stovepipe and his slender wife was scraping a deer hide in the front yard.

She looked up smiling when they reined in and set aside her knife.

Ned lowered himself carefully from the back of the sorrel, favoring his wounded side, and waited for the Cahuilla elder to speak.

'You remember my wife, Sáhat.'

'Of course I do,' he said quietly. 'How are you, Willow?'

The pretty little woman seemed pleased he'd remembered the meaning of her name and smiled up at him from the hide she'd been working on.

Then her eyes went to the bloodstain on his shirt and she rose to her feet, the wide smile suddenly slipping into a frown.

'You are hurt, Ned Gamble?'

'Just a flesh wound,' he answered. 'It was a lucky shot.'

'Yes, probably lucky it didn't kill you.'

'Now why would you say a thing like that?' He grinned.

'Hah!' she scoffed. 'We all know your reputation.'

'Aww, Sáhat.'

'Come,' she continued, sweeping her brown hand toward the front of the house, 'sit here in the shade and I will look at your wound.'

'Do what she says, my friend,' Huarache rumbled close behind him. 'Your God knows you need someone to take care of you.'

Ned nodded soberly and paced past the Cahuilla elder's little wife to the shade of the overhanging roof. He eased himself slowly down into a cane-backed chair that had seen better days and tried to relax.

Sáhat quickly kneeled beside him, pulled his shirt open, and leaned in closer to study the gash below his ribs.

'Husband,' she said softly, 'can you bring me some hot water? I'll have to clean this before we can do anything at all.'

Huarache brought a pan of hot water from the house in a matter of minutes and the little woman dipped the hem of her skirt in it. Carefully she began dabbing away the dried blood on his side.

'It doesn't look that bad,' she ventured. 'A gash, but it has stopped bleeding. I'll make a poultice of creosote and chia seeds for you.'

The Cahuilla elder stood a few yards away, talking quietly to a younger man of the tribe in their ancient tongue. After a few minutes the younger warrior ambled away and Huarache fixed Ned with a questioning gaze.

Ned ducked his head toward the house in uncertainty and spoke softly to his ageing friend's wife. 'You got any whiskey in there, Sáhat?'

She smiled up at him, warm and slow and understanding. 'Just some tulapai beer, Ned,' she answered, 'but it's fresh. That's what Huarache always drinks.'

'That'll do.'

'I'll bring you a cup,' she murmured. 'And I'll wash and mend your shirt before you leave.'

He cocked his head. 'And I thank you for that, Missus. I'm thinking I need all the help I can get.'

She disappeared inside their small house for a few moments. When she stepped back out she handed him a clay cup of the sweet corn beer.

'It will take me a few minutes to grind the chia seeds,' she said evenly, 'then we'll be able to do something for your side.'

She disappeared again and Huarache lowered himself to sit on the ground near Ned's feet.

'I am told the men who tried to kill you and the woman you were guiding stopped here to water their horses a few hours ago. It is said they seemed to be in a hurry and rode on toward the pass.'

'San Gorgonio?'

Huarache nodded ponderously. 'I'm thinking the pueblo of Los Angeles.'

'That's another two days' ride from here.' Ned groaned.

Still, he had a score to settle out there and there was no getting around it.

'Yes,' the elder mumbled. 'And that's only if you put a lot of miles behind you on both days.'

Ned frowned and wagged his head. 'It makes no sense. Those men are from Mexico.'

'Most of the people out there are from Mexico. They're the ones who settled the place.'

'But they should be heading home.'

'Home is where you make it, Ned,' the Cahuilla

elder droned. 'You know that.'

All he could do was nod his agreement, for he himself felt more at home in the wilderness than he did with a roof over his head.

He'd been through San Gorgonio Pass on his first trip to the coast and well remembered the yellowed hills with the pinyon pine giving way to scattered clumps of scrub oak and stretching all the way to the sea.

'Damn,' he mumbled, 'why does everything have to be so difficult?'

Sáhat stepped back out through the door, set another pan of hot water on the porch and shook out a long roll of calico cloth.

'Stand up, Ned,' she said evenly. 'Let's get you patched up while we still have enough light to see by.'

He did as he was told, tugged the shirt tail the rest of the way out of his trousers, and stood still while the little woman pressed a cloth-wrapped poultice to his side. She wrapped the calico cloth tightly around his ribcage, tied a wad of a knot in it, and stepped back to assess her work.

'There,' she breathed, 'that's the best I can do. If you sprinkle water on it now and again it will draw the impurities from the wound.'

'Thank you, Willow,' he croaked. 'You're a life-saver.'

She smiled broadly at his words but shrugged them off out of politeness. 'Well, I don't know about that, but at least the wound is clean.'

She rose to her feet and started toward the door. 'I imagine you men are getting hungry, and I still have to prepare something for you to eat.'

'No hurry, woman,' Huarache said quietly. 'We have much to talk about.' He dipped himself a cup of the fresh tulapai beer, leaned back against the wall and grinned.

'She puts up with a lot from me.'

An hour slipped by, two, the sun went down behind the scrub-covered hills west of them in a blaze of crimson and gold, and suddenly the stars were out.

Ned leaned back against the stout log pole supporting the overhang and gazed quietly at the birth of another desert night.

Nightfall was one of the sights he never got tired of watching, stars like chips of diamond sprinkled across the sky. Other daytime pleasures were in watching bright-breasted hummingbirds flitting from blossom to blossom, or a spindly-legged colt taking his first faltering steps and trying to figure it all out.

It grew on a man out here, witnessing the miracles God had doled out, and, somehow, it made the hardships a little more bearable.

'You should marry a Cahuilla woman and stay among us, Ned,' Huarache said quietly. 'You'd be welcome here and the woman would make you happy.'

Ned snorted softly at the elder's words. 'I don't know, my friend. I'm not so sure I could pull in double harness the way you do.'

'It isn't all that hard. You give a little and you take a little.'

'Yeah, but what if I wanted to take off for a while? Go hunting on the far side of the mountain or visit a friend who lived far away?'

'An Indian woman would understand that, Ned. As a matter of fact, if you didn't take off to go hunting once in a while she would think you strange.'

'Still—'

'Let the man be, husband,' Sáhat interrupted from the door. 'He's hungry and tired and in no mood for your babble.'

'I'm not babbling.'

'You men come and eat now,' she said flatly. 'I've roasted some porcupine meat and there is fresh acorn bread.'

Huarache grinned at him. 'You ever eat porcupine, Ned?'

'I don't think so. Be a new experience for me.'

'And so would pulling in double harness with a Cahuilla woman,' Sáhat chimed in. 'Come and eat now, while it's still hot.'

Ned followed Huarache inside the shadowed house and sat cross-legged on the hard-packed earth floor, just as the elder had done.

Flickering light from a hatful of fire reflected off the walls, casting an eerie golden glow over the room, and the air was sweet with the smell of burning pine.

'You know you can stay with us as long as you want, Ned,' Sáhat said, handing both men a painted clay bowl of meat, boiled squash, and acorn bread.

'And I thank you for that,' Ned answered, 'but I'll have to ride out in the morning.'

'Stay at least until you are strong,' Huarache murmured over his shoulder.

Ned bobbed his head in thanks and smiled at his friend. 'I wish I could, but I have to make tracks for the pueblo of Los Angeles.'

'The people who shot you?' the elder asked.

Ned nodded again. 'You already know the answer to that.'

'Then you should get some rest. I'll bring my bay mare in from the herd and you can consider her a gift.'

'Damn, Huarache,' Ned mumbled. 'I don't know what to say.'

'Then say nothing. Eat your porcupine and squash, Sáhat will make you a pad of blankets on the floor, and you can get some sleep to regain your strength.'

'And, while you're asleep,' Sáhat added, 'Huarache and I will put some things together for the trail. It looks to me like you are traveling light.'

He took a bite of the porcupine meat, a little surprised by the taste, and nodded his thanks again.

'I had a pretty good kit when I left Yuma,' he said around a mouthful of food, 'I doubt you'll be able to replace any of it way out here.'

Sáhat stood, hands planted on the flare of her

hips, and stared at him a long moment before speaking again.

'Sometimes the Cahuilla people find things along the trail, Ned, and we trade with travelers who are passing through. There is much more right here in Agua Caliente than you know.'

'Anyway,' Huarache cut in, 'let us worry about that. It's a long ride from here to the pueblo of Los Angeles and you'll be on your own. For now, it's important to get your strength back.'

'So I suppose that means no chasing Cahuilla maidens tonight and no more tulapai beer?'

'Yes, that's what it means.'

Ned huffed softly at the elder's words and grinned. 'You're a hard man, Huarache.'

The elder chuckled half under his breath and met his eyes.

'That's what Sáhat always says.'

CHAPTER THIRTEEN

Ned finished his cup of jojoba nut coffee, set Huarache's chipped clay cup down on the bench, and paced away toward the big bay horse the elder had given him.

'Old Pedro Pákash loaned me a saddle, Ned,' his aged friend mumbled, 'but he wants it back when you're done using it.'

'And I've put together some things you'll need for the trail,' Sáhat said softly. 'A plate, a cup, and a spoon. I put some food in the warbag, too. Beans, venison jerky, and some of my acorn bread.'

'I found you another coffee pot and kettle,' Huarache added. 'You left yours on the mountain.'

'Yeah,' Ned said with a nod, 'I thought about that when we were riding in.'

'There's a small bag of grounds in there, Ned, but no one had very much of the real thing.'

Ned wagged his head in awe at the couple's thoughtfulness. It was way more than he deserved.

'I don't know how to thank you for all the help,' he said quietly. 'I'm indebted to you.'

'Forget about it, Ned,' Huarache replied. 'There are no debts among friends.'

'Still,' he said, 'I feel it.'

He turned to Sáhat, smiling. 'And thank you again, little lady, for patching me up.'

She sniffed and wiped a tear from her eye. 'You don't have to say anything, Ned Gamble. I know what's in your heart. I hope you will visit us again.'

'You can count on it,' he answered. He swung up into the borrowed saddle, touched heels to the bay's flanks, and started slowly away from the village of Agua Caliente.

'And don't forget to put water on that poultice once in a while,' Sáhat called after him.

He lifted a hand to acknowledge her parting words without looking back and nudged the mare into a shambling trot along the foothills.

He had no idea what he'd find in Los Angeles. It would be a big city one day, there was little doubt in his mind about that.

The madhouse of the California gold rush was over now and businessmen from the east coast, the speculators, the shipping magnates, were gradually moving in.

The big Spanish land grants were being picked apart a piece at a time and it was pretty much accepted by everyone involved that agriculture was the coming thing for the state.

Former mountain men like William Wolfskill and

Don Benito Wilson, who hadn't lost their scalps to the Indians, had shown the way, planting vineyards and groves of orange trees in the fertile southern California valleys; now they were getting rich, selling their produce to miners.

It was something to ponder.

The last time he'd been there it had been a sprawling pueblo clustered around the old San Gabriel mission. Adobe houses and stores had risen where none had stood before. There was a maze of narrow alleys between the buildings, and he'd been hearing talk of a rough-cut *barrio* the Anglos called Sonora Town.

Killings were said to be frequent down there; knifings and cuttings took place almost every day and it was not safe for a woman to be on the streets after sundown.

Word around the campfires was that not only Mexicans were involved in the knifings. Sometimes an Anglo would wander into one of the cantinas in the little *barrio* looking for trouble, and without fail he found it.

It was not a safe place to go – for any man – yet he was sure that was where he'd find Manny Barajas and the woman, and he might not have a choice.

The woman owed him, by God – wages and half the pearls he'd dug out of the Yuha sand. On top of that was the attempt they'd made on his life.

She had been a part of it.

Even without the money and pearls, that little score had to be evened up.

He heeled Huarache's bay horse into a ground-eating canter, wanting to put some miles behind him, and tugged her head around more to the northwest. It was going to be another long day in the saddle and he was not looking forward to it.

His side still ached in spite of the poultice little Sáhat had applied to it and he rode loosely, trying to ease the pain.

The bay seemed to have a lot of bottom about her and he let her run at her own pace, feeling the growing heat of the day and the film of perspiration trickling down his back under his faded shirt.

The tans and greys of California's low desert faded slowly behind him, the crucifixion thorn and palo verde trees giving way to pine and alder in the pass.

He topped out at the summit of San Gorgonio Pass shortly before noon and reined in to give the horse a breather and a chance to graze for a while.

He stepped down from the saddle and lowered himself to a bed of soft brown pine needles covering the ground below a scraggy pinyon. He lay back on it and tugged the brim of his sweat-stained hat down over his eyes.

The pueblo of Los Angeles was still a good day's ride ahead of him and he'd already resigned himself to the fact that he'd have to camp somewhere in the hills again tonight.

The thought did not sit well with him. He'd fallen a whole day behind Manny Barajas by staying in Agua Caliente and there was no way to make it up.

Still, it couldn't be helped.

139

There were limits to what he could expect from the big bay horse and even more limits as to what he could expect from himself.

There was just no way around it.

He climbed back into the saddle after an hour, patted the big bay's neck, and nudged her into an easy canter down the long valley toward the coast.

He rode steadily the rest of the afternoon, through the stands of lodgepole pine and juniper, past the curious mule deer watching from the shadows, eventually reining in beside the shallow headwaters of the Santa Ana River just as the sun was setting.

Ned stripped the gear off the mare, staked her out in a patch of grama grass close to the water's edge where she could forage and roll all night, then wandered around the summer-yellowed hillside picking up broken scrub oak branches for a fire.

It took only minutes to put a small fire together under the pines, then he dug out the supplies Huarache and Sáhat had packed in his possibles sack.

He dipped a potful of water from the river and got a pot of coffee and a kettle of beans started before lowering himself to the blanched grass.

This would all come together tomorrow, there was no doubt about that, and his mind drifted back over the events of the past week that had put him in this position.

The woman had played him like a trout and it grated on him.

He'd always considered himself a canny man, able to read the most vacant of deadpan expressions, the vaguest of trails, yet he'd let himself be roped in by a barely believable sob story and a pair of flashing eyes.

There was a word for it, he thought bitterly . . . *stupid.*

He wagged his head at the thought, lifted the lid off the smoke-blackened Dutch oven old Huarache had gotten for him, and shaved a handful of venison jerky into the beans.

It wasn't what he wanted – not by a damned sight – but it would keep him going for another day.

The air up here was dry and carried the smell of the sea. A large flock of square-tailed cliff swallows twisted and wheeled through the gathering shadows, picking off insects flying above the river and, farther away, came the shrieking alarm of scrub jays.

The night here had a different sound from that in the desert, he decided – not as sinister, not as hazardous – and he wished he was able to relax.

It wasn't in the cards, though, and he knew it in advance.

Not with tomorrow hanging over his head.

There was just too much at stake.

CHAPTER FOURTEEN

His fire died out during the night and he had no patience for rekindling it. Instead, he splashed half a cup of cold coffee into his cup and sipped at it while he set the low-crowned hat back on his head and pulled on his worn boots.

The mare was on her feet, ears pricked forward, watching him. He had the definite feeling that she was anxious to be back on the trail; he was starting to like this horse.

He dumped the leftover beans at the river's edge, where the always hungry jays could pick at them, rinsed out the battered Dutch oven, and filled the blanket-covered canteen with fresh water.

He paced across to the bay, threw the saddle on, tied the blanket roll and possibles sack to the cantle, and swung up.

If he was any judge of distance at all he'd ride into the pueblo of Los Angeles some time after noon, into the showdown he knew was ahead of him; it couldn't come too soon.

Ned nudged the bay into a shambling trot down the wide valley, slouching back in the saddle and trying to picture the gunplay he was going to run into in the *barrio*.

There were only four of Manny's gang left now. He'd sent two of them to meet their maker back on Sheep Mountain.

Barajas himself hadn't touched his pistol up there and that was usually a sign that a man was not good with one. In Manny's case, though, Ned could also take it as a sign that his hirelings did his shooting for him.

That made the most sense.

Barajas was a thinker, a planner; that meant he'd have his defenses in order: three men to take the brunt of the fight.

Ned's only real chance would be to take them by surprise. Catch them with their guard down and take them out as quickly as he could.

Anything else meant death and he had no intention of buying the proverbial farm today.

He followed the trickle of the Santa Ana River until it flattened out and turned south, then cut west over the burned-out hills.

The smell of the salt sea air was stronger now, and he reined in atop a low rise that gave him a sweeping view all the way to the coast.

He sat the bay in the scant shade of a scrub oak tree, leaned his elbows down on the saddle horn, and surveyed the sprawling pueblo below him.

It was said the pueblo had been started by a few Franciscan padres with forty-four settlers. Now there were something like 5,000 people living there.

Seeing the size of the place, that was easy to believe.

He could make out the bell wall of the old San Gabriel mission, north-east of the settlement, the huge haciendas of well-do-do landowners on the outskirts, and the narrow alleys and adobe walls that marked Sonora Town.

That would be where he'd find Barajas and the woman, he was sure of that, and he'd need to keep his wits about him when he did.

After several long minutes he nudged the big bay forward again and rode slowly on down the yellowed slope toward the settlement, toward the gunfight he knew was coming.

Toward destiny, maybe death.

He was almost looking forward to it.

The entire horizon beyond the settlement was covered by a thick blanket of low, grey clouds and fog, which were said to be common this time of year, and he rode easily past the scattered ranch houses, the wide vineyards, and the six-bell wall of the ancient mission. He reined in at a small livery stable on the very edge of the pueblo.

As he swung down from the saddle he spotted all six of the Morgan horses Barajas had stolen from him in the split-rail corral.

Instant anger flooded his mind and he paced into the stable's little office with his fists already balled.

'Those are my horses out there, mister,' he said, jerking a thumb over his shoulder.

The grey-bearded hostler looked up from the ledger he was tallying and narrowed his eyes.

'Not by God likely,' he rumbled. 'I bought them hammerheads yesterday and got a bill of sale to prove it. Paid cash on the barrelhead for 'em, I did.'

He tapped the dottle out of a well-used corncob pipe and didn't look away.

'Mexican guy name of Manny Barajas sell them to you?'

'That'd be the one.'

'Figures.' Ned nodded. 'It was him got them away from old Frank over in Yuma.'

Grey-beard tilted his head curiously at his words. 'Frank Dougherty?' he asked evenly. 'How is that old maverick?'

'You know him?'

'Well, I hope to shout I do,' the old hostler crowed. 'Came West together, we did. Me and him, the Sublette brothers, and old Broken Hand Fitzpatrick. Trapped with Ashley's Hundred for many a year.'

He picked up an unwashed enamel cup, spilled half a cup of black coffee into it, and fixed Ned with flint grey eyes.

'We came down here in twenty-seven with Jedediah Smith and them. Then, when the fur trade went sour, Frank stayed on at Yuma Crossing and I drifted out here. How's he doing, anyway?'

'He's dead,' Ned droned. 'Barajas killed him

145

when he stole my horses.'

'Dead?' the grey-beard blurted. 'Well, I'll be damned.'

Ned lowered his gaze to the straw-covered floor of the stable and spoke with a rare reverence in his voice. 'Good friend of mine, old Frank was, and it's a little hard to believe he's gone under.'

The ageing mountain man wagged his head. 'Well, I'll be a moss-back mule. I always figured him to be ninety-five years old and get shot by a jealous husband.'

'Yeah, that sounds about right for old Frank.'

'Stand you to a cup of coffee, sonny?' the ageing hostler asked. 'I got a notion that maybe we should talk.'

Ned nodded. 'Coffee'd be good and I could probably use some advice right about now, too.'

'Drag up a chair and take a load off, then. Ain't had me a chance to talk to a real *hiveranno* for quite a spell.'

He thrust out a work-hardened hand and grinned. 'I'm John Randall, by the way. Most people know me as Shoshone John.'

'Ned Gamble,' Ned replied gripping the hostler's hard hand.

Randall nodded soberly. 'Heard of you,' he said. 'Heard you know your way around the desert as well as any redstick walking on two legs.'

'I've been out there a time or two.'

He picked another of the old-timer's unwashed cups off the cluttered desk, poured himself a shot of coffee, and scooted a rickety cane chair up next to the desk.

'You want to tell me about it?' the old mountain man mumbled.

'Not much to tell, really,' Ned answered. 'I was guiding a Mex woman into the Yuha badlands, looking for treasure. When we found it that Manny Barajas and his men come drifting out of the brush. Shot me up, stole the treasure, and rode off with the woman.'

'That be the good-looking filly that was riding with them yesterday?'

'Reckon it was,' Ned replied. 'Seemed to me like the whole thing had been planned out ahead of time and they were all in it together.'

Shoshone John huffed at his answer. 'Damn me if I don't hate devious people. Just ain't no call for it.'

'I'll drink to that. You got any idea where this Barajas might be?'

'More'n likely down in Sonora Town,' the old liveryman muttered. 'You know what they say about birds of a feather. You going after them?'

'I have to, John,' Ned told him. 'They owe me. Any hotels down there?'

'Only one I know of is the Casa Bodega down on Calle Corta. About a block this side of the church and turn right.'

'I'll try it,' Ned mumbled over the rim of his cup. He pushed himself erect, set the cup back on the cluttered desk, and started for the stable door.

'You watch your topknot out there, young feller,'

the old mountain man said to his back.

Now it was Ned's turn to huff. 'Funny, that's exactly what old Frank told me.'

'Good man, Frank was. Give you the shirt off his back and never fault you for needing it.'

'Yeah,' Ned said, stepping into the saddle, 'and I'm going to even the score up on that one, too.'

'Keep the faith, coon,' Shoshone John rumbled. 'Mayhap we'll be seeing each other again.'

Ned touched heels to the big bay's flanks, walked her slowly out of the old mountain man's stable, and cut his eyes to the southwest, trying to get a feel for the pueblo.

Truth be known, he'd never felt comfortable in towns and avoided them whenever he had a choice.

This time, though, he didn't have one.

Manny Barajas was somewhere in the little *barrio* sprawled out ahead of him and it was time to pay the piper.

He rode in slowly, past the squat adobe buildings, keeping his eyes fixed on the cupola atop the massive stone block wall of the old plaza church.

A three-legged dog lapped water from a puddle at the side of the street and, somewhere in those low adobe houses, a baby cried.

It was no trick finding the Casa Bodega, a block this side of the church, just as old Shoshone John had said. A weathered adobe building, it set in the middle of the block with red-painted railings. Flower vines trailed down from earthen pots on the second-floor balconies.

He swung down from the saddle, wrapped the
bay's reins around the stout hitching rail, and
stepped up on to the porch fully aware of the
curious gazes he was getting from people along the
street.

The shallow lobby of the Casa Bodega had a red-
tiled floor, hallways leading off to rooms on either
side, a flight of stairs just to the left of the scarred
counter, and the air smelled of dust.

The slope-shouldered clerk behind the counter
looked to be half-asleep, his black hair was tousled
and his shirt was not quite tucked in, but he opened
his eyes quickly enough when Ned stepped through
the door.

'Dolores Torreón,' Ned rumbled. 'Which room?'

The clerk gave him a condescending smile and
planted his hands flat on the counter. '*Perdóname,
señor*. I'm not at liberty to give you that information.'

Ned took a deep breath and blew it out slowly,
fighting to keep his composure.

'How old are you, *compadre*?' he asked quietly.

'Forty-one. Why?'

'Would you like to see forty-two?'

'Well, of course I would.'

Ned nodded soberly. 'Good. Then I'll ask my
question again.'

He reached forward with his left hand, grabbed a
fistful of the clerk's shirt, and pulled him forward
against the counter.

With his right hand, he dragged the long-barreled
Colt Peacemaker from its holster, jammed it hard

against the man's nose, and eared back the hammer.

'Dolores Torreón,' he said a little more forcefully. 'Which room?'

The clerk's breath caught in his chest and he went suddenly wide eyed. 'Room twenty-one, *señor*. Right at the top of the stairs.'

'Show me,' Ned muttered. 'And don't even think about raising a ruckus.'

He led the slightly-built clerk out from behind the counter, shifted his grip to the back of his collar, and steered him toward the stairs.

There was no sound of footsteps on the floor above them and they went up quietly, careful to make no noise of their own on the dark mahogany steps.

'You want me to call her out, *señor*?' the clerk asked in a hoarse whisper.

'I want you to stand right there and keep your mouth shut up,' Ned said, nodding toward the wall.

His eyes went to the brass number 21 tacked on a red-painted door and he took another cautious step.

He tapped lightly on the edge of the door, then stood cautiously to the side. He'd seen gunfire come blasting through a closed door in the past and it was never a pretty sight.

'*Quién es*?' came the muffled voice from inside. 'Who is it?'

Ned tapped lightly again and waited in silence.

After a moment he heard the soft footfalls from inside the room, clamped his teeth hard together, and his whole body was tense.

The instant the door cracked open and he saw the dark eyes peeking out he kicked it and went in with the Peacemaker already leveled.

The room was furnished with a table and chair and a heavy-looking armoire against the wall, The windows were hung with cheap chintz curtains. The thick adobe walls had been plastered over and white-washed and there was an ornate crucifix tacked prominently to it just above the rumpled feather bed.

The impact of his kick had knocked Dolores Torreón back on her pampered ass and she looked up at him from a braided throw rug almost in panic.

'Ned!' she blurted. 'Wha. . . ?'

She tried to cover a blackened eye and the scab forming on a split lip but wasn't quite fast enough to hide it from his view.

He couldn't have cared less.

'Where's Manny Barajas?'

She lowered her gaze to the floor at his question and he could barely hear her answer.

'He's gone.'

'Gone?' he demanded. 'What the hell do you mean, "he's gone"?'

'He took the pearls – even the six I had in my pocket – and walked out.'

'He left you in the lurch?'

She looked back up, studying his face. 'Yes.'

He lowered the Peacemaker and stared at her.

That she'd been smacked around was obvious, and he had a hard time wrapping his mind around

151

the concept of a man beating a woman. It just wasn't done.

At the same time he wondered what she could have done or said that would warrant that kind of treatment.

It had to be something that would absolutely enrage a man and, other than questioning his manhood, he had no idea what it could be.

'Just out of curiosity,' he mumbled, 'what was the connection between you two?'

'He . . . he was . . .' she stammered, 'my fiancé.'

He snorted loudly at her confession, but somehow, it all made sense now.

They'd been in it for the money, for their own future, and the sob story about the family ranch in Jalisco was as phony as a wooden nickel.

'Well, I'll be damned,' he muttered with the hint of a grin spreading across his desert-dark face. 'So let me understand all this. You double-crossed me and he ended up double-crossing you? Now doesn't that take the biscuit?'

'It isn't funny.'

'It is to me, lady. Funniest damned thing I've heard in weeks. Does he have the pearls?'

She wagged her head sadly and averted her eyes again. 'I was told he traded them to Don Pedro Salazar for title to a land grant in the state of Guerrero.'

'Any idea where he is now?'

'Probably in that little cantina on the corner, but he won't be there long. I was also told that he booked passage on a ship back to Acapulco. Supposedly they will be leaving on the outgoing tide this evening. Are you going after him?'

He hesitated only a second before answering, 'I have to. The sonofabitch owes me.'

'Yes,' she moaned. 'He owes me, too. A great deal.'

'That's your problem, lady. As far as I'm concerned, you and I are all done.'

He turned on his heel and marched out of the shoddy room, seething with anger at all the deceit, all the double-dealing.

The little cantina on the corner, was it?

Without a word he paced down the stairs, unwrapped the bay's reins from the hitching rail, and led her down the dusty street.

He knew exactly what lay ahead of him now, and it was far too late for words.

CHAPTER FIFTEEN

The cantina on the corner didn't look like much, a flat-topped adobe structure with rafter poles jutting out of the sides and battered batwing doors hanging on leather hinges.

The sad strumming of a guitar and the refrain of an old Mexican folk song came drifting out to the street just as he stepped up to the porch.

'*Cucurrucucú, paloma.*

'*Cucurrucucú no llores.*'

The singing stopped and a sudden hush settled over the place the instant he pushed through the sagging doors, almost as if every man and woman in the room was aware that a gringo had just stepped in.

For a Wednesday afternoon the place had a good crowd: farm workers, ranch hands, and a few shifty-eyed characters who were probably dodging the law.

He noted the narrowed eyes of a few customers

who were leaning down on the counter nursing their whiskeys but ambled in anyway. There was little else he could do.

Four men hunkered over a cluttered card table in a shadowed corner of the room, trying to read some telltale sign in the other players' faces, and half a dozen more had bellied up to the bar.

The air inside was heavy with the sour odor of perspiration mixed with cheap perfume. A thick pall of grey cigarillo smoke hung like a shroud below the ceiling.

The only movement was at the cluttered card table, where three of the men rose to their feet, wary and on guard, and spread themselves to the left and right.

Only Manny Barajas with his hooded eyes and carefully trimmed mustache remained seated, peering at him with venom in his eyes.

The half-breed Yaqui took a pace forward, glowering at him, his hand hovering near the butt of his pistol.

'You looking for something, *amigo?*' he slurred.

Ned Gamble didn't answer. Just drew and fired.

The slug took the half-breed high in the chest, jerked him backwards, and he crashed down on the rickety table.

Cards and coins, half-empty shot glasses and a dirty ash tray spilled noisily on to the puncheon floor of the cantina. The customers behind him either bolted for the door or threw themselves down behind quickly upturned tables.

155

Several shots whined through the air at that instant and Ned, too, dove for the floor.

Another shot plowed into the floor at his shoulder, sending an eruption of wood splinters into his cheek, and he rolled quickly to his right.

He swung the Peacemaker to the left and squeezed off another shot into the slab-sided *vaquero* he'd heard Barajas call Paco back on Sheep Mountain.

Paco grunted once and dropped as if he'd been pole-axed.

A young-looking pistolero standing next to Barajas brought his six-gun to bear a little too slowly and Ned's shot took off the side of his face. He, too, was jerked backwards a step or two, leaving a smear of blood where he slid down the wall.

Only Manny Barajas himself was left, an evil grin spread across his pinched face as he braced his Colt Army revolver up with both hands and aimed as if he wasn't really familiar with guns.

Ned swung the Peacemaker yet again, lower and to the right, pulled the trigger . . . and the goddamned thing jammed!

Manny's grin widened at the clacking sound Ned's pistol had made and he pushed himself to his feet. He looked to be thoroughly enjoying the moment when he would at last get to kill the desert rat they'd lured into their scheme, the heavy-shouldered man who was now scrabbling around on the floor in front of him, waiting to die.

All he had to do was pull the trigger.

Ned grimaced, trying his damnedest to spin the cylinder of the Peacemaker and knowing in his heart he had only seconds left to live.

Time seemed almost to stand still as he glanced again at the poison in Manny Barajas's eyes.

Barajas opened his mouth to speak, probably some spur-of-the-moment insult, but the sudden thunderous roar of a .50 caliber Sharps buffalo gun shattered the silence that had settled over the cantina and the insult remained unspoken.

Manny Barajas was slammed violently back against the wall, dead before he hit, and slithered down to slouch beside the young *pistolero* with half a face.

Ned jerked his head round quickly and spotted his new acquaintance, the old-time mountain man, Shoshone John Randall, standing in the doorway, calmly feeding another round into the long-barrelled Sharps' chamber.

'That was for old Frank Dougherty,' John rumbled. 'And this one's for me.'

He squeezed off a second deafening shot into Manny's chest, even though it was painfully obvious to everyone in the cantina that the fancy-dressing *vaquero* was very, very dead.

'Yes, sir, by God, old Frank Dougherty was a long time friend of mine and I don't take kindly to people killin' off my friends.'

A shadow came up behind Shoshone John. Ned, knowing the Peacemaker wouldn't fire, could only shout a warning.

'Behind you, John!'

The old hostler spun quickly at his call but it was only Dolores Torreón coming to see the aftermath of the gunfight, the outcome of all the treachery.

Shoshone John stepped aside, eyeing her suspiciously, but let her pass without saying a word.

She stood just inside the doorway for a long minute with her fists doubled, scanning the bodies on the floor – who was dead and who only injured? – before her gaze settled on Ned Gamble, just then forcing himself to his feet.

She sauntered slowly to his side, her skirts swishing as she moved, and fixed him with those huge, flashing black eyes of hers.

'Are you all right?'

He didn't respond. Instead he lifted his eyes to the old mountain man still standing in the doorway. 'You saved my bacon, John.'

'Glad I got here in time to help,' came the mumbled reply. 'I'll be gettin' on back to the stables now. Looks like you two might have somethin' you need to talk about. Come see me before you ride out, *hiveranno.*'

'I'll do that,' Ned answered.

Shoshone John turned, pushed back through the beat-up batwings, and Ned heard his footsteps thudding away on the boardwalk outside.

He looked around at Dolores Torreón and narrowed his eyes.

'You've got some kind of brass following me down here.'

'Please, Ned,' she purred, 'can you help me? I

have nothing left.'

He stared at her for a long minute, not quite believing his ears, then shook his head. 'I don't think so, lady. You made your bed and now you can lie in it.'

'But what will become of me? Will I be someone's mistress? A common whore?'

He wagged his head. 'I couldn't care less what happens to you. I'm not normally a vindictive man, but you brought this on yourself and I've got no sympathy at all for you.'

'Please,' she said. 'I don't know who else to turn to.'

He squinted at her, considering everything that had taken place in the last week, and there was no humor in his voice.

'Well, let me see now,' he mumbled, 'you lied to me, you cheated me, you got me beat out of my Morgan horses, any hope for the future, and a whole lot of men have died because of you. Why in God's name would I help you now?'

'Because you're Ned Gamble, the desert rat, and you don't know any other way.'

Ned exhaled heavily at her words. 'That is probably the only thing you've ever said to me that rang true.'

He reached into his pocket, pulled out a handful of coins, picked out one that he slid back in, and dropped the rest into her hand.

'Here,' he said leveling his eyes at her. 'That's all I've got. I'm holding one back for a shot of snakehead whiskey before I ride out of here. And damn me if I'm *still* not living on bacon and beans.'